Finn

Hops & Hugs…distilled with danger!

Bradley Farm Series
Book 3

MARY JANE FORBES

Todd Book Publications

FINN
Hops & Hugs...distilled with danger!

ISBN: 978-0692585702 (sc)
Printed in the United States of America
Todd Book Publications: 11/2015
Port Orange, Florida

Author photo: Geri Rogers
Cover design 2018 by Angie: pro_ebookcovers

Books by Mary Jane Forbes

Bradley Farm Series
Bradley Farm
Sadie, Finn, Jeli
Marshall, Georgie

The Baker Girl Series
One Summer
Promises

Twists of Fate Series
The Fisherman, a love story
The Witness, living a lie
Twists of Fate

Murder by Design, Series
Murder by Design
Labeled in Seattle
Choices, And the Courage to Risk

Novels
The Mailbox
Black Magic, An Arabian Stallion
The Painter
The Baby Quilt ... a mystery!
The Message...Call Me!
Twister

House of Beads Mystery
Murder in the House of Beads
Intercept
Checkmate
Identity Theft

Short Stories
Once Upon a Christmas Eve, a Romantic Fairy Tale
The Christmas Angel and the Magic Holiday Tree
RJ, The Little Hero

Visit: www.MaryJaneForbes.com

Snippets from the Amazon cloud:

The Baby Quilt ★★★★★ **Great read,** September 28, 2015
I had to keep reading as I loved the story and couldn't wait to find out what was going to happen. A lovely ending.

Murder by Design ★★★★★ **excellent story,** September 17, 2015
Loved the storyline and the characters. Didn't like it ended. Would recommend. Plan to get next book when I see it

Murder by Design ★★★★☆ **Murder By Design,** September 3, 2015
I liked the book. It had a little bit of everything. It kept my interest and I liked that it had family values and great friendships in this mystery book.

Sadie, Bradley Farm ★★★★☆ **A must read! Have a glass of wine and enjoy!,**
August 17, 2015, Bradley Farms, a terrific series. They just keep getting better. Each visit with the Bradley's becomes more enjoyable and interesting than the one before. Just could not put Sadie down. Really enjoyed the reading.

Bradley Family Tree

Marshall Bradley
1810-1880

|

Kenneth Bradley
1845-1920

|

Mason Bradley
1896-1946

|

Arnold Bradley
1927-1970

|

Daniel Bradley
1951-

Offspring—Danny and Jane Bradley

Twins
Sadie & Marshall
|
Finn
|
Jeli

Wolfe's son
Georgie

Finn

Hops & Hugs…distilled with danger!

Chapter 1

THE BATTERED RED TRUCK pulled to a stop at the back entrance of the Cock & Feathers Tavern. Sighing, Finn turned the ignition key, the engine quivering to a standstill. Wrapping his arms around the steering wheel, he rested his head on the worn leather.

Outside the June air was crisp and sweet. The fragrance of nearby pine trees drifted in the truck's open windows, as did the chirping of the birds welcoming the advent of summer. But Finn wasn't singing. Far from it. He had signed divorce papers not an hour ago, stuffing the envelope in the mailbox slot on his way to work. It was four years to the day since his wife declared she didn't love him, and wanted a divorce. No more living on the meager wages of his part-time jobs she said, most of which he squirreled away in a savings account, an account to fund his current dream. She'd had enough.

Where is my dream of a brewpub now, he wondered?

Last night he confided to his parents the dream that had been building in his mind for months. His pops came up with words of encouragement for the new idea. His mom also encouraged him. Maybe this plan would be the big one.

He had too many dreams … dropping the one for the allure of the next. He never seemed to follow through. Now, he found himself living back at home—Bradley Farm, two-hundred acres nestled in the rolling hills of Lakeville, New Hampshire. Back working as a bartender at the Cock & Feathers Tavern, a bar owned by Louie Tuttle, a friend.

Lifting his head, Finn removed the key from the ignition, climbed out of his truck, and locked the doors. Setting his small-brimmed, straw cowboy hat on his head, he curled his fingers around the sides, curving the edges in place—his carefree, affable bartender look. He paused, gazing at his reflection in the truck window. A trim cut to his thick black hair, a piece tied in the back into a pigtail. A slight edge of sideburns along his cheeks joined the five o'clock shadow he couldn't shave away for more than an hour. A hint of a mustache grazed his upper lip.

"Time to paste a smile on your face, my man. Time to play the happy bartender." *Yep,* he thought, kicking a small stone to the side. *The man behind the bar who listens to a guy stopping off for a cold beer on his way home, or, a man's tale of woe which usually involved a girl, or, a girl drowning her sorrows after a breakup, the guy choosing someone else. I should charge for the therapy sessions.*

Once in awhile, the man's story was a happy one—a new girlfriend in tow. Finn smiled, *a girlfriend would be nice.* A genuine smile crossed his face at the thought of a girl to talk to. The only person in his life he talked to, the only person he was close to, was Georgie, a surrogate brother since the day Finn was born. Georgie knew all about his dreams. Georgie was always ready to help with the next idea that popped into Finn's head.

Straightening his red neckerchief, he tucked the red plaid shirt inside his jeans, hitching them up around his trim waist. Stiffening his spine, opening the weather-beaten door to the back of the tavern, he strutted into the dimly lit backroom.

He paused at three keg-like containers, one yellow, and two stainless steel with tubing strung from one to another, checking the progress of his latest try at a distinctive brew. Satisfied, he continued through the door, walking by the galley kitchen behind the order window, turning into the back of the bar. As bartender, this was his domain.

The old tavern was once a general store nestled in a stand of stately pines. Louie preferred the word tavern to bar. He thought of it as an old English pub. That way he got by with minimal renovations, leaving the brick walls and beamed ceiling. He did spring for two large television screens—one above the bar, the other on the far wall. On Saturday and Sunday afternoons the patrons shuffled the small square tables to suit the size of their group. In another hour, the tavern would fill with Red Sox fans. The Sox were scheduled to play against the Yankees.

Red and white checkered oilcloth hid deep scratches on some of the tables. Others were left bare. Soon the smell of burgers on the griddle, curly fries in the fryer basket, would tickle noses, as fans whooped and hollered for their teams in the sporting event of the day. Mixing with the sport's junkies was the latest hot tune from the jukebox, or an oldie—Billy Joel moaning over a lost love. At times, all vied for airtime.

Decades-old, wide-pine floorboards were flanked in front with a bank of multi-paned windows facing the street. Some would call the windows quaint, English-pub like. Whatever you called the windows, they added a touch of charm. All in all, the Cock & Feathers was a cozy place for the regulars to hang out. They were always greeted by the charismatic bartender who called them by name from their first visit. Finn prided himself on his name recall.

When the evening slowed, he was known to pull out his guitar from under the bar. He played country songs, once in a while singing, but more often than not just strumming the melody encouraging the patrons to add a karaoke rendition.

"Top of the afternoon to you, Louie. Where's Jenny?"

"Some bikers showed up. Nothing I couldn't handle. That is until prissy missy quit."

"Jenny quit? I thought she liked her job, liked mixing it up with the guys."

"Sure did and mixed it up with one of them all right. Told me she was quitting, and left on the back of a motorcycle with a ponytailed man old enough to be her father." Louie pushed his black rimmed spectacles up on his broad nose, a thick fringe of salty hair ringing his bald head. He toddled his diminutive, five-foot plump figure up to the grill, a fresh, white bib apron covering his ample belly.

"What are we going to do, Louie? We need a waitress. I can't—"

"Stick a sign in the front window. That's the best we can do for today. If no one applies, I'll put an ad in the Weekender. Now, get out there. You'll have to double as bartender and waiter. I'll take the orders as usual at the window."

———

AT FIVE O'CLOCK SHARP, she walked in.

Finn's heart seized. She was the prettiest woman he had ever seen. She wasn't a young kid ready to hop on the back of a ponytailed biker. No, she was like him—thirty something. This woman had class—the way she walked, walked right up to him, smiling at him across the bar as she hitched up on the barstool. Blonde waves framing her face spilled over her shoulders.

"Hi, there. What can I get for you?" Finn said touching the brim of his hat in greeting.

"The sign in the window ... you're looking for a waitress?"

"We sure are. Do you—"

"I want the job. I have experience. I'm reliable, and can—"

"Hold on. Let me get Louie. He's the boss. I'm sure he'd like to talk to you ... Miss?"

"Kathleen. Kathleen O'Leary."

"Well, Miss O'Leary ... is it Miss or Misses?"

"Miss. Can I bother you for a glass of water while you tell Mr. Louie I'm applying for the waitress position?"

"Sure thing." Finn stuck a glass under the water faucet, added two ice cubes, and set it in front of Miss O'Leary. "Louis Tuttle is my boss's name. Just so you know, he likes to be called Louie. He owns the tavern."

"Oh, sorry ... I just assumed ... thanks for the water."

"My pleasure. I'll be right back, Kathleen. Do you mind if I call you Kathleen?"

Kathleen shook her head as she took a sip of the ice water. Kathleen was fine with her.

"You can call me Finn," he said, a sparkle returning to his dark brown eyes over an easy smile.

Kathleen's eyes followed him around the corner, seeing him reappear behind the order window. He whispered in the ear of an older man whose eyes barely cleared the sill of the window, both men glancing over at her. A flush rising on her face, she turned away.

The bald head moved away from the window, then appeared again behind the bar, and stood in front of the woman who said she wanted the job of waitress in his tavern.

"Miss O'Leary, hello. I'm Louie. Finn says you're looking to be our waitress?"

"Yes, sir."

"I haven't seen you here before. Live near?"

"Down the road, sir."

"You have experience?"

"Yes, sir. At a Howard Johnson's bar." Kathleen dug around in her shoulder bag. Inching off the barstool, she stepped to a table, rooting around in the bag. She retrieved a brush and a lipstick. Stuffing them back in the bag, she looked up at Louie. Sorry, I must've left the telephone number at home."

"Tell you what, Miss O'Leary—"

"Kate. Call me Kate."

"Okay, Kate, Finn and I are in a bit of a jam. Our waitress quit on us this morning. She ..." Louie sighed, "*She* doesn't matter. Could you help us today? If it works out between us, you've got the job. If it doesn't, we'll pay you for the day."

"Thank you, Louie. Yes, I can start right now. Wore my traveling shoes."

"Traveling shoes?"

"Yes sir, traveling from the bar or kitchen to the customer. How late are you open?"

"Ten or twelve—depends on if we have some hangers-on or not."

"I just have to make a call. Then I'm ready."

Louie stuck out his hand. "Welcome, Kate. Finn, show Kate the backroom. Clean off a place for her to put her things and give her one of those white aprons—the frilly one that ties around the waist. Make your call, Kate, then join Finn at the bar."

"Thanks, Louie," Kate said following Finn to the back. Removing a crate of onions off a small table for her shoulder bag, he handed her an apron.

"Come out front when you're ready. I'll go over our various beers on tap, and the bottled brews we carry," Finn said. "Most of the guys, some girls, usually want a cold beer from the tap ... along with free pretzels. The regulars will know you're new. If they ask for something you're not familiar with ask them to point it out on the menu, or give me a nod."

———

KATE HAD RACED HOME, dressing for the part of a waitress after she saw the sign in the window. Her waitress costume consisted of a slightly above the knee black skirt, white short-sleeved blouse, and white sneakers. She needed the job and was going to try her darnedest to get it, be ready to accept on the spot. After making her call, she tied the apron around her waist. Sucking up a breath of air, she was ready to take her position at the end of the bar.

Finn explained the routine with a chuckle. "Give me the drink order, and Louie the food order. That's about it."

Finn's dark brown eyes sought her light blue. If you asked him the color of her eyes, he would have said the color of the lake at the back of Bradley Farm on a bright sunny day. A smile spread over his face. *Yup, she sure is pretty. And all that sir stuff. Very respectful.*

He tore his eyes away and stepped to a couple who entered the tavern taking a seat at the bar. The man ordered two beers on tap. Tipping each glass, Finn filled the glasses, with a nice head of foam. Sneaking a peek at Kate several times, the foam ran down the outside of the second glass. She giggled as he wiped the glass clean then set the glasses on the bar in front of the couple along with a small bowl of pretzels.

———

A LITTLE AFTER SEVEN O'CLOCK, there was a lull in the action. Louie hustled out to the bar. "Kate, if you have a minute, can we talk?"

"Sure thing," Kate said following Louie to a side table.

Louie nodded to a chair and sat across the table from her. His black eyes peered out from the round glasses held with thick black frames. He was a comical character with his big grin and bald head fringed with tufts of hair. "You're terrific, Kate— definitely qualified. So, would you like the job?"

Kate grinned. "Yes, I would."

"Good. Now, tell me what kind of hours you're looking for—"

"As many as you can give me, Louie. I have a commitment on Sunday, but all the other hours would be great. I need the money … ah, what's the pay?"

"Oh, oh. A commitment on Sunday? That's a busy day here— big sports day on television."

Finn was listening to the conversation, watching as he cleaned up behind the bar. He thought he saw a flash of panic cross Kate's face.

"I'll, I'll make arrangements … I'll, I'll make it work, Louie," Kate stammered.

"Still, that's a lot of hours, Kate. I doubt you'd—"

"I can do it. As I said, Louie, I need the money. I'm dependable, not a clock-watcher—"

"How about the first week at four bucks just to be sure, a probation period. Then, $6.25, plus tips, of course. Today can be the first day of the probation period."

Kate smiled back at him. Her big blue eyes merrily looking about, taking in her new work place, visualizing the past few hours, the flow of patrons sitting at tables, others up at the bar swapping quips with the bartender who kept glancing her way.

"Do I have to split my tips with anyone? The bartender? You?"

"Oh, no. Tips are all yours."

"Okay, Louie, provided I get a raise if I do well … after the first month."

"If you do well, and the regulars have good things to say and refer friends, then I can swing a raise … a slight raise."

The hours sped by. At 11:15 Kate hung up her apron, picked up her shoulder bag and said goodnight to Louie and Finn. Finn watched her through the side window. The parking lot was empty except for his truck and Louie's old Chevy coup. He stepped closer to the window catching sight of the new waitress pedaling away from the bushes, disappearing down the street out of the white light shining on the sign—*Cock & Feathers Tavern.*

Finn wouldn't let her do that again. A pretty woman like Kate riding a bicycle at this hour wasn't safe. He'd offer to drive her home.

Chapter 2

Bradley Farm Kitchen

SIR WINSTON THE THIRD or fourth, Finn couldn't keep track as one rooster replaced another, let out a cock-a-doodle-do that was not to be ignored. Opening his eyes, he gazed around the bedroom he had grown up in. Little had changed except for the walls—rocket ships to blue plaid wallpaper, to soft lime-green paint. At thirty-five years old he was back home at the farm. The melancholy from the previous day returned. He didn't like the feeling.

His mind traced the downers that kept haunting him—a failed marriage, and the unfulfilled dream of someday opening his own business. There were other hiccups on his life's journey, but a new image chased the downers away. Not far away—a few moments to a bright spot several days ago that brought a smile to his lips. Kate O'Leary. Louie's new waitress. She could brighten anyone's day. She was nice, pretty, and had an easy way with the customers.

Adjusting the elasticized waistband on his green and white checkered pajama bottoms, Finn untangled his feet from the sheet, planting them on the braided rug. He needed a project to escape his funk. Worse than a funk, depression had set in. He shook his head, muttering, as he stepped to his dresser and looked in the mirror. "You have a project, dummy. You started a business plan. Not a brewery, a brewpub. It's sitting in your dresser drawer."

Finn loved the farm, but what he really wanted was his own place. His eyes darted to the laptop computer on the desk where he had done his homework through grade school, high school, and two years of vocational school—farming. Pops told him, if he couldn't decide what he wanted to do with his life, then he should at least learn the latest techniques in farming. Of course, what Pops didn't realize, there wasn't much farming going on at the moment. Flower beds and herb plants slated to be sold at the farm's garden shop didn't count as farming. The shop was one of his mom's profit centers, except the so-called profits were slim. After his divorce, and moving back into the farmhouse, he would have done anything to help his parents.

His intention to become a bartender was to save half of his earnings for a brewery while experimenting with brewing techniques. He insisted he pay something for room and board, but his mom wouldn't hear of it. She told him to give his idea a year to materialize. If it didn't work out, then they would discuss the matter again. His baby sister, twenty-nine year old Anjelica, nicknamed Jeli, still lived at home but was making plans to move out once her interior-and architectural-design career kicked in—any day now, she kept reminding him. And then there was Gran, Pop's mother. She had a room on the first floor, a suite with a bathroom and sitting area. She was a spry seventy-eight.

Shaking the thoughts from his head, Finn's eyes returned to the computer. Several weeks ago, a Sunday morning, he and Pops were watching television, the HGTV channel. Several episodes aired, one after the other, on a new craze—tiny houses, a twist on recreational vehicles, better known as an RV. Kids graduating from college with big student loans to pay off were buying the tiny houses, parking them on their parent's land, or RV parks, neighboring farmland, anywhere they could get a good deal with utility hookups available. The tiny houses were of various sizes, but one in particular caught Finn's attention—twenty-four feet long yet the width fit on the road so he could trailer it without a special permit.

It could be fun to buy one of the builder's barn-raisers. Finish it yourself the website stated. A barn raiser was built on the trailer bed at the company site in Colorado—flooring, studs, roof. Heck, Finn had lots of help available for such a project. Georgie would love it, and Pops said he could perform the woodworking easy as pie with his experience refinishing antiques and building new furniture. Georgie and Wolfe, his dad, remodeled the tree house they lived in on the back of the farm's acreage. In comparison, a tiny house would be easy.

Finn felt a new spring in his step as he trotted down the stairs to breakfast. If his nose was right, Gran had a griddle full of her buttermilk pancakes on the stove. He kissed his mom, a hug for Gran, and then he poured a cup of coffee and sat with the three men of the family sipping coffee around the harvest table.

"Okay, young man, what's put that sparkle in your eyes?" Wolfe asked.

"Remember a couple of weeks back when we all saw the television show on tiny houses?"

Gran placed a platter of hot pancakes in the center of the table just as Jeli, rubbing her eyes wandered into the kitchen, throwing kisses to the group as she shuffled to the coffee pot.

"Couldn't forget that, son. A fine piece of woodworking, and so clever how they used every inch of space," Pops said.

"I've been in touch with the company … several times. I think I'm ready to invest in one of their houses."

"Finn, I thought you were happy in your old room upstairs. What's changed?" his mom asked. Without saying anything, worry lines crossed her face. Was her son ditching the brewery idea for a tiny house?

"Mom, you know I've been thinking about starting a brewery, in fact I have a few gallons fermenting in a back room of Louie's tavern. He said the backroom wasn't serving anything useful except as a place to stash stuff."

"I don't understand, Finn," Wolfe said. "Are you planning on setting up a brewery in the farm's big barn near the road or at Louie's?"

Finn and Georgie exchanged glances. Georgie knew what was coming. The pair were close. Shared most secrets, and his plans for a tiny house was one of them. He poured syrup over his pancakes, waiting with a grin as to where the conversation was leading.

"The barn is still the number one choice. But, I've expanded my business plan—a brewery and pub and a place of my own to live close to the barn to keep an eye on the operation. Right now I need my job, plow the money into the execution of my plan for a house. I'll either go the frugal route, or all in. Frugal is my first choice."

"You're talking in circles, son. Just come out with it. Your mom and pop can take it."

"If I go the frugal route, I'd ask for your help, Pops. Ask for everyone's help actually. See, I can save a boatload of money if I invest in one of the builder's barn-raiser deals. They build the house of my choice, the skeleton, on a trailer—roof, sides. and floor. I ... we do all the finishing work, buying materials as we need them, and voila ... a tiny house."

"What's the all-in version, Finn?" Gran asked.

"I finance the house—they build it, trailer it to the farm or the tavern, and set it up. Really, all they would do is unhitch their truck."

"Where are they located?" Jeli asked, her eyes bright, beginning the interior design of the tiny house—colors, wood, lighting.

"Colorado Springs."

"You've been talking to them … pictures?" Jeli chimed in again, her step a bit stronger to the coffee pot for her second cup.

"Thought you'd never ask. Hang on." Finn's muscular frame flew out of the kitchen, his feet pounding the over one-hundred-year-old wooden stairs up to the second floor … a slight pause, then pounding back down to the kitchen. He laid out a fistful of pictures, floor plans, and testimonials from owners of a tiny house. They told their experiences in building a house themselves out in Colorado under the watchful eyes of the company's builders, or building it from scratch on their land. The company provided the plans and a list of materials, or the company framed the house on a trailer—the barn raiser."

"Look at this one, Janie," Pops said to his wife, placing a picture of a tiny house with red shutters in her hand. "Cute, huh?"

"Hold on," Georgie said. "Let me get these plates out of the way. Knives and forks on top please."

"Oh, I love this one," Jeli said. "All these notes on the back, is this—"

"You have a good eye, Jeli-bean. Your design instincts are right on. This is the model I want. It's twenty-four feet long and can be hauled with a truck like mine."

Finn didn't see Wolfe and Danny roll their eyes—Finn's 1942 Ford truck traveling across the country and back hauling a house?

Finn didn't miss a beat. "I've saved enough for the deposit, but I think I'll apply for a loan to cover the cost of materials as I need them. What do you say?" Finn looked around at the group. If they agreed to help, he could go with plan A—a barn-raiser. If not, he couldn't see doing it himself. Pops, Wolfe, and Georgie were the carpenters in the family, something he wasn't very good at. When he pounded a nail, his thumb always got the worst of it.

"What do you think Gran, Jane?" Pops asked.

"I say let's support the boy," Gran said reaching across the table to pat her grandson's hand. "I'll make sure you worker-bees have plenty of fresh water, coffee, sandwiches … whatever."

"Wolfe? Georgie?" Pops said, grinning at the pair.

"We were in from the moment he said tiny house. After all, it's only a tad smaller than the tree house that Georgie and I remodeled. So how hard can it be?"

"When do you want to start, Finn?" Georgie asked.

"If you all think it's a good idea, I'll call the builder today. I figure, to save the cost of delivery, Georgie and I can drive Big Red to Colorado and pick her up. Meet the staff, get some tips."

Danny smiled. He had courted Jane in his red truck, which he called Big Red. His son carried on the tradition, coming home a few months back with his red truck. There were a few dents, a little rust, but he was proud as a peacock—rust, dents, and scratches. Here was another of his son's crazy ideas. The boy had spirit. He was glad to see his son was beginning to come around after the trauma of his divorce. Now, if he could just finish this project.

Chapter 3

———

STARING AT THE COMPUTER SCREEN, finger hovering over the mouse, Finn's heart double ticked. The form for the down payment on the tiny house barn raiser was complete. All he had to do was click *Send*.

Adam's apple quivering, his finger hit the mouse button.

An immediate replay displayed. "Thank you for your order. We will contact you tomorrow with delivery information."

A nervous grin spread across his face. This was a project he was going to complete. No if, or maybe. He had been the butt of numerous jokes from the family as they sorted through the pictures spread over the kitchen table—are you sure you can squeeze through the front door, will you fall over the edge of the loft without a railing, do you really want to live in a doll house for little girls? Are you secretly building it for Louie? The tiny house would be a wonderful house for the chubby, five-foot tavern owner.

The ring of his cell brought Finn back to earth.

"Hello, Mr. Finn Bradley, please."

"I'm Finn Bradley."

"Great. This is Cameron Foster from the tiny house builders. I'll be your contact, Mr. Bradley."

"Wow, this is fast."

"Yes, we know our customers are anxious to hear from us. The sales department just forwarded me your order. I'll be the builder framing your house on the trailer bed. On the form you checked the box that you'll be picking up your barn raiser. Going over your order with my shop manager, he estimates your house will be ready for pickup in two weeks. Is that convenient?"

"Yes. I think so. I have to check with my friend. He'll be making the trip with me."

"If there is any change on our end, or a change at your end, we can reschedule the date. I'm calling to introduce myself. If you have any questions, please call, or send me an email. I've sent a confirmation of your order along with all the details of your purchase. You can contact me directly using my email address or the company address included at the bottom of the confirmation."

"There is one thing, Cameron. My friend, Georgie, and I would like to meet with you in the shop. We'll be staying a couple of days so we can soak up all the tips you can give us."

"Not a problem. When we get closer to the date, I'll confirm your arrival and set up some time in the shop. Now, you have a good day and congratulations on your purchase of our barn raiser. By the way, you chose one of our most popular models."

Finn stuffed his cell in his pocket and raced out the door to find Georgie.

Chapter 4

———

FINN WAS LATE FOR Kate's first day on the job as a full-time employee. She had finished the probation period with flying colors. With the excitement of sending the purchase order for his house, time got away from him. This also meant that he was late prepping the bar.

He popped in the back door of the tavern with five minutes to spare before opening at 11:30. Louie had already reviewed the menu with Kate—burgers, dogs, fries, coffee—short and sweet. Alcohol, with a few exceptions, was limited to beer—ales, lagers, stouts. There were varieties of each available, but regulars were content with their favorite on tap, or in the bottle. Louie was ready if they ordered a burger on the side with all the fixings. However, Louie kept a fine bottle of Johnny Walker scotch for his old-timer friends. Finn's specialty at the Cock and Feathers was a Bloody Mary cocktail, with or without vodka, served with a plume of celery.

With no customers as yet, Finn asked Kate to sit with him at a little table at the end of the bar. It was time to learn more about the pretty waitress with blonde waves and big blue eyes, eyes that mesmerized him. She was so cute in her black short skirt and white blouse, and those white sneakers skipping over the pine floorboards.

"I've seen you … on your bicycle. Do you live far from here?" he asked leaning forward.

"Umm, two or three miles. It only takes me a few minutes, and it's a way to keep my weight under control."

Finn kept his mouth shut. There was nothing wrong with her weight. Petite with plenty of curves. "Do you have a car? Or, are you planning to ride your bike home when we close?"

"I can borrow a car, but I'd rather ride my bike. It doesn't take long."

"Kate, it's not very safe to be riding your bike late at night. When I'm here, which will be most nights, I'll give you a lift. Throw your bike in the back of my truck—"

"Really, Finn, I'll be fine, but thanks anyway." Kate grabbed her order pad to help the first customer of the day, leaving him with his mouth open.

Finn pushed his hat up. So, she didn't accept my offer. Worse, she seemed annoyed I suggested it wasn't safe. Well, Miss O'Leary, I'm going to watch out for you whether you like it or not.

Chapter 5

———

ONE DECISION LED TO another dilemma. Finn was struggling on how he was going to tell Louie about his house and ask for time off to go to Colorado to fetch it. During the mid-afternoon lull, he decided it was as good a time as any to tell Louie about the tiny house.

He and Georgie had mapped out the route to Colorado Springs. They took into account that his truck couldn't be pushed over the speed limit and the strain on the engine during the return trip towing his house back to New Hampshire. Figuring how many days he needed, factoring in spending some time at the factory, twelve days probably was the minimum to bank on—two thousand miles plus fifty to Colorado Springs. Georgie had whistled—*that was a long way.*

Tracing the route on the map, the only good thing Finn noticed was that the mountains were on the western edge of Colorado Springs. They would only have to deal with some big hills, and lots of flat land, so maybe Big Red could handle it. On the bright side, he and Georgie always managed to persevere, coming out of a jam on top ... most of the time.

With two of them driving, taking brief rest periods, they could drive straight through, maybe stopping one night. Definitely stop more nights on the return trip, dealing with the fear of losing the house on the road.

Finn leaned against the wall watching Louie clean the grill. He had decided to hit it head on.

"Louie, I need some time off, ten days, maybe twelve, a couple of weeks."

Louie looked over his horn-rimmed glasses, up and down at Finn. "Well.......okay. What for?"

Finn had struggled with how much to tell Louie about his plans. The tavern owner knew that he was experimenting in the backroom brewing beer. Maybe he even surmised Finn would ask to include a good batch on tap at the bar. But Finn had never really divulged that one day the two might be in competition. Well, he would cross that hurdle in the future ... when he had to.

Louie had been very good to him, truth be told. Took him under his wing at a low time in Finn's life, going through the divorce, and Finn didn't want to lie.

"You know I'm back at the farm. I can't afford a regular house, so I thought a tiny house might be a good investment. Have you seen them on TV? They're creating quite a buzz."

"Sure, I've seen 'em. Before I fixed up a couple of rooms over the tavern, I was thinking about it myself. I decided it was cheaper to scour and paint upstairs."

"That's why I'm buying a barn raiser—really saves money. The builder erects the structure on a trailer bed and I take it ... well, Pops and Wolfe take it from there ... with my help of course ... and Georgie's."

Louie shot a look at Finn. "You're not quitting on me are you?"

"Oh no, no, Louie," Finn said, inching his hat down over his eyes. He quickly pushed it up, a toothy grin on his face. *Maybe he would ask Louie to be a partner in his new brewery. That's right, a partner would be a great idea.*

Chapter 6

―――

AFTER FINN'S REQUEST for time off, Louie returned to cooking burgers. Nothing more was said and Finn only had to wait to hear from the builder for a date when his barn raiser would be ready for pick up.

As the sun shed its remaining beams of light, a man sauntered into the tavern, glanced around, his eyes adjusting to the dim, brick interior. A string of white lights outlining the order window to the left, behind Finn's domain, sent a soft glow across the bar. Kate had introduced candles on the table tops and was in the process of touching a lighter to each wick. The flickering flames added a bit of fun, punctuating the gathering shadows in the tavern.

The man ambled to the bar. Settling on the high barstool, the heels of his scuffed boots slid onto the foot rest. The brim of his black Stetson shadowed his face. A turquoise stone mounted in gold hung on the bolo tie around his neck. The turquoise was a stark contrast to his black shirt, open a couple of buttons at his throat, revealing tufts of black chest hair matching his brows and upper lip.

Smiling at the newcomer, Finn set a coaster in front of the man.

"What can I getcha?" Finn asked.

"Your best stout."

"We have—"

"You choose. Fancy names don't mean nothin to me."

"You got it."

Finn filled a glass with rich, dark-brown beer, topping it with a head of foam, setting it in front of the man. "Anything else? Burger? Dog?"

"I'm looking for a friend. He likes to hang out in bars. Likes to work in bars. Thought you might know him."

"What's his name?"

"Bulldog," the man said, followed with a hearty laugh.

"A big guy?" Finn asked.

The man laughed again. "Nah. Winnie Bulldog … you know, after Winston Churchill because he's anything but. Bulldog also likes fat cigars." The laugh eased into a smirk. A deep scar down his left cheek twitched, accentuated with a shadow from the tiny lights at the back of the bar.

"Nobody around here goes by the name of Bulldog, big or small. Hang on a minute. Let me ask the boss if he's ever heard of Bulldog."

"You do that, sonny. And I think I will have one of those burgers. A thick one. Rare. Loaded, if you know what I mean."

"Onion?"

"Loaded!" The man's eyes drew to slits, challenging Finn to ask another question about the meaning of loaded.

Finn caught Kate's eye, nodding, as he left the man's order on the spike at the window, that he was leaving the bar.

She acknowledged the signal, nodding back.

Wiping his hands on the towel tucked under his belt, Finn hustled behind the order window to ask Louie if he ever heard of anyone by the name of Bulldog. Louie wasn't at the grill, so Finn continued through the swinging door to the backroom.

Finn walked in letting the creaky door swing shut behind him. A bare light bulb hung in the middle of the storage area with cases of beer, kegs of beer, and a door to a small refrigerated room holding a few more cases of beer, packages of hamburgers, hot dogs, and buns. Finn's experimental brewing apparatus was tucked in the far corner.

He found Louie sitting on a crate of onions, elbows on his knees, hands on either side of his cheeks holding his head. His little black eyes magnified behind the thick glasses. A streak of burger grease crossed the bib of his white apron.

"Louie, you okay? You don't look so good. Do you want me to ask Kate to fix a burger order?"

"Sure. Sure. That's a good idea. You do that."

"There's a man out front. He's asking about a man going by the name of Bulldog. Wondered if we ever heard of him."

"What did you say?"

"What do you mean, what did I say. I've never heard that name before. You?" Finn chuckled. "Supposedly, the nickname came from Winston Churchill. Go figure."

"No. Tell him no," Louie said in a low voice, almost a whisper, his eyes darting around the room.

"Sure, Louie." Finn looked down at his boss, his *short* boss. "I'll ask Kate to cook him up a burger. Did you check out the grill with her? The fryer?"

"She can do it."

"Did you see him walk in?"

"I did."

Do you know the man, Louie?"

"Sorta. Everyone calls him Scarface cause of the gash..."

"Yep, I think I've heard the name from Pops." Finn continued staring down at Louie. It was obvious he was troubled, troubled approaching scared stiff. Sucking in a deep breath, releasing it slowly, Finn shoved the door open, pressing his heel back against it as he stepped through closing his boss into the safety of the backroom.

He passed Kate cooking, adding three hotdogs on the grill. Finn slowed his gait as she nodded at the man with the hat. She had taken care of him. Returning behind the bar, Finn saw the man had cleaned his plate leaving a smear of mustard on the rim. His lips were pinched as he stared down at a coin he twirled between his thumb and forefinger, letting it flop on the counter.

Again, he twirled the yellow-colored coin. The hologram on the backside gleamed with each spin.

The man sensed the bartender had returned and was staring at him. Without looking up, the scar-faced man asked Finn a question. "Ever see one of these—a bitcoin?"

Finn shook his head. Kept his mouth shut, deciding he'd play along with the stranger. He'd seen an image of a stack of such coins on Louie's computer screen upstairs. He was playing poker on the internet, a cigar butt smoldering in a tin ashtray next to the keyboard. Louie went into a long explanation of the currency.

"This pretty little thing is worth $260.95 the last time I checked this morning. O'course, that fluctuates second by second."

"Where do you buy such a coin, if it's real that is?"

"Oh, my friend, this is real. You open an account on a currency market-exchange website and then transfer money from your bank account to the exchange. Transfer enough to cover the going price of the coins plus an exchange fee. Now, if I wanted to sell this coin, I can also do that through the exchange. The reverse then happens, I ship the coin, and the cash is deposited into my bank account."

"Sounds tricky ... and risky."

"Can be. But most people who use or deal with the coins don't buy the physical coin, such as this one. They keep an account of virtual coins. Virtual currencies, such as bitcoins, have grown globally. There are believers who think it is a better and faster way to buy things, or to play games, gamble, anywhere in the world. Others think it will cause a disruption in the banking system."

"I guess you think it's okay."

"Bitcoins have been around since 2009. You can buy stuff anonymously. Many small businesses like them for international buying and selling because they aren't tied to any country, aren't subject to regulation—no credit card fees." The man chuckled again.

"Are there a lot of them in circulation ... bitcoins?"

"Physical ones—no. Virtual bitcoins—yes. They're the world's biggest cryptocurrency. Most people don't bother with this pretty little thing. They deal in digital bitcoins, virtual currency," the man said, pocketing the coin.

"So, one bitcoin, as of this morning, is worth $260.95, give or take the fluctuation?"

"You got it. They've been as high as one thousand dollars for one coin, then settled back down to around what I told you. That's why investors buy them—hoping for a killing. The early adopters certainly made a killing." He chuckled again. "The first investors bought one bitcoin for a nickel."

"Wow, that would be some return on an investment."

"Yup. That's why I want to find Bulldog. I heard he was one of those early investors, has some bitcoins that he wants to sell. I'd hate to see him lose out. Well, I'll be on my way. Thank the little lady for the burger. It was mighty fine."

Bitcoin

Chapter 7

———

THE ROAR OF A MOTORCYCLE followed the scar-faced man's departure as night descended. Finn hustled to the front window, watching, a chill running up the hairs of his arms.

That man is trouble, he thought.

Turning away he looked for Kate, catching her eye behind the order window. A group of five had parked their Harleys—they were strolling into the tavern laughing. Finn moseyed behind the bar as Kate left the grill to take the bikers' orders. At the same time, Louie peeked out of the backroom. Taking a few steps, his eyes darting around, he quickly took his place at the grill.

"Two pitchers of #5," Kate called to Finn. Turning to the order window, she called out to Louie. "Five burgers with fries."

Louie nodded, flashing a tentative grin.

Finn sighed. Everything was back to normal as if the scar-faced man had never been there, except his empty glass remained on the end of the bar, the plate with a smear of mustard alongside.

Kate took five glasses to the group along with napkins. She returned to Finn picking up the pitchers of beer.

"Kate, let me drive you home tonight. If that is alright?"

"Okay," she said, glancing up at him, then quickly walked with the pitchers to the group whooping it up with another round of laughter. They had moved a table to get a better shot at the dartboard mounted on the wall.

FINN LAID KATE'S BIKE on the bed of his truck. Taking her hand, he helped her up into the cab, then climbed in the other side behind the wheel. She put her tote on the floor between her feet, an apron tie poking out of the top. Leaning over, she stuffed it inside. "I have to wash this in the morning."

Finn smiled at her remark. He didn't care what she said. He liked hearing her voice. "Left out of the parking lot?"

"Yes. I'm just three miles down. A white house on the left. Thanks for the lift, Finn. That man kinda spooked me."

"I know what you mean. But let's forget about him. You live so close, but I've only seen you riding your bike once before, except for at the tavern, and believe me I'd remember."

Kate smiled but didn't look at him. "I've only been here a few weeks. Staying with friends for awhile ... renting a room."

"Renting from a friend?"

"I insisted after I landed the job at the tavern."

"Where are you from?"

"Wisconsin. I take it you're a Bradley from Bradley Farm?"

"You got it. I'm a bartender by trade, I guess you'd say. But I grew up believing I'd be a farmer. It's not that I don't love farming, but I don't dislike it either. What I loved growing up was working the farm with my pops. Pops was hurt in the war so it was hard for him, not much stamina. So he had to rest. Often. That's when the fun began—me and Pops, he telling me stories about Grandpa Arnie. We spent hours together out in the fields. Pops was a steady Eddy. But Grandpa had a wild side, at least when he was a young buck. That's what Pops said Grandpa would call himself, a young buck."

"Nice you're close to your family. I grew up in foster homes— me and my sister."

"That must have been tough. Is your sister here with you?"

Kate looked out the truck's open window, a soft breeze caressing her cheek. "No, she isn't."

"What did you do ... before you came to the tavern? I'm so happy you decided to stay. You'd better not leave," he said, glancing at her with a broad smile.

"I don't plan to leave, at least not for awhile. But you never know. Did you go to college? I always wanted to."

"I did. Took the same major Pops did—agriculture, latest methods of farming. But I really want to start my own brewery, so Pops said I'd better get some experience at a bar first. Pops came from a long line of Bradleys. He inherited the farm from his father, and so on back to 1840. But when Great Grandpa Bradley died, Grandpa Arnie immediately worked to bring his dream come true—raising racehorses. Pops told me about going with him to the track with a stallion or a beautiful filly. He reminisced on the races won, and not much time on those he lost. Grandpa Arnie died young ... in his forties. Yup, Pops and I were a pair when I was growing up. I was by his side, sitting on a hay bale when he told me the stories of Grandpa Arnie."

"So much history. I miss that ... history. Turn into the driveway just ahead."

Finn slowed down, turned in at a modest, white cape-style house. The front porch was dark. Turning off the engine, he turned in his seat leaning back against the door. Kate did the same, comfortable with each other.

"Tell me more about Bradley Farm," Kate said.

"Well, as a kid I wanted to be just like Grandpa Arnie which meant sticking to the farm. However, Bradley Farm is no longer listed in the Who's Who of horse racing stock. When Grandpa died, Pops sold all but two of the horses. Gradually, Mom's been transforming the barns to other businesses—a farm stand with fresh vegetables to start, then a barn with antiques and holiday decorations. She even sold Christmas trees that Grandpa Arnie planted for a rainy day."

"Do you have brothers? Sisters?"

"Oh, now that is a change in the family history. Farmers usually had big families, but none of the Bradley clan had many children. Two at most, from what I've been told. Mom and Pops had twins right off the bat. A great story. The twins were conceived on their wedding night—Sadie and Marshall. Then me, I'm considered a middle child. Last is the baby of the family, Anjelica. We call her Jeli."

"Baby?"

"Twenty-nine now. Lives at home trying to find her niche in the world. Looks like interior design, with a minor in architecture may stick. Then there's Georgie. He and his dad live with us. Georgie is like a brother … four years older than me. Oh, wait, I have to tell you about my upcoming adventure."

Kate giggled at his sudden burst of enthusiasm.

"I'll be taking two weeks off, maybe as soon as next week."

"What're you going to do?"

"I, young lady, am going to pick up a tiny house. Have you heard of them?"

"Actually, I have. But I've never seen one. They sound like they'd be cramped."

"Not at all. It's amazing how much space there is when you plan wisely. Georgie and I are taking Big Red here, that's what I call my truck, to Colorado to pick up what the builder calls a barn raiser. The builder frames the house on the trailer bed ready for all the finish work."

"Amazing. Where are you going to put it?"

"On the farm next to a barn. The barn where I may start a brewery someday. But that's between you and me … and my family of course. I don't want to worry Louie. He's like a sweet uncle. I'd never hurt him."

"You have a lot of plans, Mr. Bradley. I'm excited for you."

"Kate … can I call you Katie? You are a perfect Katie with your blonde hair and big blue eyes. Have I told you I'm glad you came to work at the tavern?"

"Yes, you have," she said giggling again. "And, yes, you can call me Katie. I like the way you say it. Now, I have to go. It's getting late. Can you stand my bike next to the porch?"

"Sure. Hold on. I'll come around and help you down. The first step is a killer."

Finn hopped out and removed her bike from the truck. He opened her door, and held up his hand. She grasped his hand and slid off the seat. He was ready for her falling against him. She felt as good as she was pretty.

Kate quickly regained her footing and stepped back, pushing a strand of hair behind her ear. He thought she stepped away a little reluctantly but maybe that was wishful thinking on his part.

"This was fun, Katie." He leaned in giving her a peck on the cheek.

"Yes, it was. Thanks again for the lift. See you tomorrow." She hurried off to the back of the house. Seconds later a light came on in a back window, then off.

"Yup, you sure are pretty. I want to know more about you, Katie O'Leary," he whispered to the stars.

Chapter 8

———

FINN WAS A HAPPY man over the next few nights. Kate was going to be close, sitting beside him in the truck, chatting, his heart pole vaulting in his chest. It had become routine to give her a lift home after the tavern closed. But tonight was different. He and Georgie were leaving for Colorado early tomorrow morning, and he missed her already.

Parking his truck in the driveway where she was living, he let out a sigh. As the previous nights, the windows were open allowing a warm breeze to circulate, but tonight the crickets were silent adding to his gloomy feeling. Finn tossed his hat behind his seat, as they both removed their seatbelts, twisting around, leaning against the truck's doors.

"The customers like you, Katie. A lot. I think business is picking up because of you."

She laughed. "It's the beginning of summer, silly. Everyone's looking for a cool retreat from the heat that's coming, not to mention the Red Sox baseball games. I met the college student who's going to tend bar while you're gone."

"You are right, we lucked out with him. The guy applied at the farm for a summer job. Georgie thought he might be a good fit to help Louie at the bar while I'm away. After I get back, he'll work the rest of the summer on the farm … always lots of odd jobs, chores, helping customers in the garden shop."

"I know Louie is relieved to have the help."

"Have you ever ridden a motorcycle?" Finn asked.

"Yes, a few times. Why?"

"I have a Harley. It's in Louie's shed right now. Would you like to borrow it while I'm away? I think it would be safer than your bicycle … while I'm away."

"I'll think about it …"

"Louie has the key … he'll help you."

"Umm, I could certainly outrun … get away from—"

"Do you like it here, Katie—the tavern, New Hampshire?"

"I guess so. A job is a job … no, I'm sorry. That was a flip answer. I do like it here."

"You must be about Jeli's age … twenty-nine? Ever been married … if it's too personal, you—"

She laughed again. "I wish I was twenty-nine. I passed thirty-two a few months ago, and, no, I've never been married. Close but …" She left her answer hanging.

She left a lot of his questions hanging, but he didn't care. He figured she'd fill in the details when she was ready.

Finn reached over, traced the top of her hand lying in her lap. Her skin was smooth, soft and warm. "I was married. Four years. My divorce is final … took almost a year. My ex couldn't take being poor. I put the bulk of the money I earned into savings to start my own business, like I said, a brewery. Looking back, we were wrong for each other, saw things differently I guess. We were young."

"You have so many plans. I just hope I can get through the day. One day at a time, that's the extent of my plans."

"Do you have a cell phone?"

"Yes. I …"

"Let's exchange numbers … that is if you want to. I can text you on my wild journey to Colorado."

"I'd like that." Katie searched around her tote, pulling out a piece of paper and a pen. Writing her cell number, she then handed the paper and pen to Finn. "Here. Tear off a piece and write your cell number. I can tell you what's going on at the tavern ... whether that spooky man came back. How long did you say your trip will take?"

"No more than two weeks. Hopefully less, and hopefully Big Red doesn't break down. Georgie and I will be meeting with the builders on how to finish my barn raiser—"

Kate leaned forward patting his hand. "Big Red won't let you down. I'm sure of it."

Her touch was magic, sending tingles up his arm.

Kate drew her hand back.

Finn's eyes went from warm to way warmer.

"I have to go in. Thanks again for the lift."

Finn clambered out to hold her door open. Taking her hand, she jumped down. He caught her, wrapped her into a brief hug with a quick peck on her lips. He wanted to hold her longer, wanted to keep his lips on hers longer, but he didn't dare. No way did he want to alarm her. Slow and easy ... he wanted to know more ... and he sure didn't want her to leave the tavern because he was being too forward. However, he couldn't help himself, and chanced the little kiss.

"I'll be in touch, Katie. I sure would like to know how you're doing, too ... not just tavern stuff. Will you text me back?"

"Every time you text me I'll text back. I promise." A smile lit up her face in the moonlight. On tip toe, she gave him a quick kiss on the cheek, and then hurried away into the house.

Finn didn't move, couldn't move, didn't want to move. He waited for the light to go on ... and then off.

A puff of air escaping his lips, he turned and climbed into his truck. Tomorrow was a big day. He wished that Katie was going along with them.

Chapter 9

———

THE SEND-OFF COMMITTEE lined up alongside Big Red. Finn and Georgie stepped down the line giving hugs, and receiving words of encouragement for a safe trip from Wolfe, Pops, and his mom.

Hopping into the old 1942 Ford, the white hood looking like it was slathered with sunscreen. Finn let her roll down the driveway, then gave her some gas as he turned east heading to Interstate 95. The pair whooped and hollered, slapping the outside of Big Red's doors, waving out the windows as the send-off-committee faded in the distance.

"Coffee?" Georgie asked with a big grin.

"You bet, brother. Who woulda thought, Georgie? You and I going on a great adventure, headed west like our country's settlers. But, unlike the pioneers, we're bringing my little homestead back to New Hampshire. I can't imagine traveling in a covered wagon can you?" Finn said laughing.

"I don't know. You may feel like a pioneer in that new, very small, house of yours."

Finn shot his friend a grin, then turned his eyes back to the road.

"Just sayin. You've only seen pictures," Georgie said. "Could be different up close and personal, as they say."

Finn may not have looked like a pioneer but he was in costume—straw hat, red neckerchief, and plaid shirt tucked into his jeans. Both men jammed their feet into their well-worn cowboy boots. On the farm you had to be ready, never knowing what you might step in. Georgie rarely wore a hat, but asked Danny if he could borrow the dark brown cowboy hat perched on a peg in the old horse barn.

Thinking about his surrogate parents, always brought a smile to Georgie's face. "You go right ahead, son. Artie would be proud to see you start your travels in his hat," Danny told him.

The miles clicked away, dropping quickly into Massachusetts.

"Hey, thanks for cleaning out the barn, clearing a spot, a workshop for the tools and supplies we're going to need to finish the house."

"Not a problem. Did you see the painting Dad and I found wedged in back of an old hay wagon? I showed it to Danny. He thinks it goes back to that ruckus with the Scarpetti family, when they were nose to nose. Danny and Scarpetti, both wanted the painting that had hung over the farmhouse fireplace in the living room for decades," Georgie said.

"I know all about that. It was appraised and Scarpetti ended up paying Mom and Pops what it was worth. Mom needed the money bad for the farm at the time, and Scarpetti wanted the painting. Turned out both sides got what they wanted. So Wolfe thinks the one you and he found in the barn may be worth something?"

"Could be."

"Maybe we'll hang it in the brewery, or in Louie's tavern. A painting would give one or the other place a certain panache. My new word from Jeli. I didn't know what the word meant but I guessed it was something good if Jeli said it. Looked it up—a certain flair, or style. I don't know when I'm going start the brewery and I'm already decorating it." Finn chuckled, following the highway signs to New York. "I thanked Wolfe for checking out Big Red. He said he made a few repairs but didn't promise we wouldn't break down somewhere between here, there, and back. I sure love your dad, Georgie."

They settled into a comfortable silence, a long-friendship kind of silence, as Big Red cruised down the highway.

After a quick stop for gas, a couple of sandwiches and sodas, they were back on the road. Before they knew it they were on Interstate 84 West, crossing into Pennsylvania. Both were relieved to be out of the traffic around the outskirts of New York City. Finn glanced at Georgie. "What about we drive through the night, if we can? I figure we'll spend the second night in Kansas, a motel off the road. Then it's a straight shot to Colorado."

"Okay by me. We'll arrive fresh, sort of, at the tiny house company. But we have to take it easy coming back. Stop every night. I've never hauled anything like a house before. I'm sure it will be tricky ... nerve racking," Georgie said.

"Hey, there's a truck stop ahead. I could use a large coffee plus we need gas," Finn said, maneuvering into the far right lane.

"You got it, partner. I'll get the coffee, while you get the gas."

Finn filled up Big Red's tank while Georgie bought the coffee, four cheese burgers, and two packs of moisturized wipes.

The farm boys, turned cowboys, switched the country music station on high as Finn pulled out of the truck stop. They sang along with Glen Campbell's, *Galveston,* and thumped their thighs to Glenn Miller's, *65-oh-oh-oh.*

Georgie opened the spigot of Finn's coffee, handed it to him along with three napkins and a burger. Leaning back, he opened the other coffee and took a long sip. "How was Danny?"

"What?"

"Back at the truck stop, I saw you on the phone. Figured you were giving the folks a trip report."

"Oh. I called Kate."

"Oh, oh. You've mentioned her, but calling her first on our great adventure—"

"Just wait until you meet her. I think I've found *the one*."

"*The one*, like the one in trying the marriage department again?"

"Well, not right away. She doesn't know it, and I sure don't want to spook her. She's had a tough life—foster parents. She and her sister. In Wisconsin."

"Do you have a picture of *the one*?"

"No. I messed up. Should have taken a picture with my cell before we left." Finn hit the steering wheel leaving a smear of ketchup.

Georgie laughed, opening a pack of wipes. "Here, wipe that wheel before I take over."

"How about you, Georgie, ever meet someone special? You've never brought a girl to the farm. At least, not that I know of."

"One or two. Kept it private. The librarian at the town library … we had a few coffees, a couple of lunches, and a dinner. She helped me with some research I was doing on crop rotation for the farm. For awhile I thought she might be *the one*. But she made it plain that I wasn't *her* one."

"That's too bad. But, best not to get hitched and then find out you weren't right for each other. Believe me, divorce is *nooo* fun."

Georgie stared out the window, his fingers tapping his thigh. "Dad and I found something else in the bottom of an old piece of luggage. A Baptist Hymnal from Savannah. It had an inscription— *To Rosemary, God speed*. What do you make of it?"

"First Sadie finds a picture in the attic of the farmhouse. Rosemary is written on the back. And now a hymnal with her name again and both found in a very different place on the farm. I don't know what to make of it."

They sat in easy silence, munching their burgers.

"Georgie, does Wolfe ever talk about your mother—who she is, or where she is? I mean, the crazy story of him walking up the driveway of Bradley Farm carrying you, a baby in a basket, is really weird."

"I agree, it is. I haven't pressed him about my mother … seemed to be too painful for him to talk about her. He did say she was of Spanish descent. I presume that's where I got my beautiful olive skin," he said laughing. "I guess she left us. I used to fantasize her as a gypsy, something exotic." This time he didn't laugh. Turned his head instead, staring out the window.

Finn flashed a look at his best buddy. He couldn't imagine not knowing his mother, not knowing any of his family. He made a mental note to ask Kate about her foster parents. *God, I hope they weren't mean to her … and her sister. Wonder what happened to her sister. With no other family, it's strange that Kate would up and leave her.*

———

"HEY, THERE'S THE SIGN for Interstate 80 West," Finn said transferring lanes. "Ohio coming up. Thought we'd never be done with Pennsylvania. When we spot a place for dinner let's go in. We both need to stretch our legs."

"Sounds good to me. I wasn't sure you were ever going to stop." Georgie was presently the co-pilot, switching with Finn when he needed a break from the wheel. The copilot was in charge of the map detail.

After a relaxing pit stop—fresh coffee, and splitting a steak dinner so they wouldn't get drowsy with a full stomach, and ordering sandwiches wrapped for the long night ahead—they were back on the road.

Before they left, Finn sent a text to Kate.

———

12:05 a.m.
Hi. We R making good time!
How R U? Sleeping?
I miss those blue eyes.
Finn.

12:11 a.m.
Hi back.
Can't sleep.

Worried about U on road with that relic U call a truck. Please, please, text me when U arrive at C.Springs. Kate.

Chapter 10

———

THE CO-PILOT HAD to stay alert. There were many highway changes through Ohio.

"Finn, you're sure we don't have to go over the Rocky Mountains? I mean that would not be good with Big Red pulling a house on a trailer, I don't care how tiny the house is."

"Don't be a worrywart. I was told the road from here is open plains for miles and miles."

Georgie refolded the map, folding behind where they came from, only showing where they were going.

Both found it peaceful driving under the stars. Traffic was light with only an occasional semi-trailer truck passing them. A tanker truck driver, hauling milk, tooted his horn in greeting as he left Big Red in the dust.

Finn merged onto I-70 W, crossing into Indiana.

By three o'clock the next day, after numerous pit stops, gas ups, and many more sandwiches, they crossed the border into Kansas, Finn pulled into the first motel he saw. Bone tired didn't exactly describe how they felt. After a dip in the swimming pool, a beer, and a pulled pork sandwich, they flopped down on the twin beds without even saying goodnight.

In the morning, they rose with the sun anxious to get to Colorado Springs. Stopping at a diner for a cup of coffee, they hopped in Big Red, ready to finish their journey west.

Georgie kept an eagle eye on the map. Neither engaged in conversation. It was beginning to feel like it was taking forever, feeling like they would never get there. "Good news, bro. Sixty-seven miles and we'll be in front of the tiny house company."

———

GEORGIE OPENED AN empty sack for Finn to toss in the sugar-coated wipe from the sticky buns they picked up earlier with the coffee. "Only a couple more miles and we turn off the highway," Georgie said his index finger resting on the map.

"Let's celebrate. Stop at the first ice cream parlor."

"Only if you buy," Georgie said, grinning.

"Oh, no you don't. It's rock, paper, scissors, bro. There's a Dairy Queen."

Parking in front of the ice cream shop, the two jumped out of the truck and stretched.

Finn, nodded at his fist resting in his palm. "Ready?"

"Ready," Georgie said.

The pair locked eyes.

Finn grinned.

Georgie grinned back.

The two big boys thumped their fists on their open palms.

Georgie opened his palm—*paper*—ready to wrap around Finn's rock. As kids Finn always showed a rock.

Not this time.

Finn opened two fingers in a V-shape. "Sorry, bro. My scissors cut your paper. Make that a double scoop of rocky-road … with sprinkles," he said, punching Georgie's shoulder.

———

ICE CREAM WITH SPRINKLES gone, hands wiped, Finn grinned peering out the windshield.

"Look at that sign, Georgie. Tiny Houses, two miles ahead."

"Are you excited? I know I am. I wonder what it's going to look like—up close and personal," Georgie said.

"You betcha, I'm excited and a little nervous. I can't hit a nail straight."

"Don't worry on that end. Dad and your pops are pros, and yours truly is pretty good too. I can do more than sit behind the wheel of the tractor, you know."

Finn nodded, flashing a grin at his companion. "Thanks, Georgie, for coming with me. I might have chickened out."

"You're welcome, bro. Let's check in to the motel Foster arranged. Freshen up for our rendezvous with a tiny house. Yahoo!"

Chapter 11

Finn's Barn Raiser

CAMERON FOSTER WAS A tall slim man, with dark brown skin and a shaved head. Seeing the red truck with a white nose pull into the parking lot, he hustled out to greet his new buyer. He knew the next day and a half would be thrilling and terrifying for him.

"Hello, Mr. Bradley, I'm Cameron Foster." Foster stuck out his hand to Finn, the two men pumping a hearty handshake.

A broad grin across his face, Finn introduced Georgie, who received the same enthusiastic handshake from Foster.

"How was your trip?" Foster asked.

"Long but uneventful," Finn replied.

"Glad to hear it." Foster turned. "Come on, guys, follow me."

Finn and Georgie fell in line to the back of the parking lot curling around a large building.

"Here she is, Mr. Bradley, your barn raiser. What do you think?"

Finn, wide-eyed, stopped in his tracks. It may be called a tiny house, but standing in front of the green structure on wheels, it seemed monstrous. *What was I thinking? Hauling a grasshopper the size of a dinosaur back to the farm … two thousand miles?*

A whistle escaped his lips. "She's bigger than the picture, Mr. Foster, and forget the Mr. Bradley. Call me Finn, and my friend, Georgie," Finn said, his arms folded over his chest like a proud papa.

"And I'm Cameron, or Cam. You're saving a lot of money by purchasing a barn raiser, Finn. After you take a peek inside we'll tour the factory. You may want some add-ons. Included in the price, as you can see, is the framing and the green zip-board sheathing, roof, and flooring built and fastened securely on the trailer. All that is taken care of, and your trailer is equipped with brakes, lights, and underside flashing. Also included is temporary protection from ice and water."

"It's summer, Cameron. Let's hope Georgie and I don't run into any ice storms on the way back to New Hampshire," Finn said, chuckling. "Can we go inside?"

"Sure thing. You go ahead. I'll follow, explain what you're looking at. We installed your front door, painted red, the color you picked. As you'll see, the sub-floor is fully insulated. Walls and roof are framed."

Again, Finn was thankful Georgie was with him. Georgie kept a level head and it didn't hurt that he had a photographic memory. Finn on the other hand hopped from one subject to the next, asking a question and, in his excitement, forgetting the answer the next minute. Georgie knew his friend well, and was ready with his iPad to take notes, asking Foster to repeat if he didn't get something exactly right.

Inside, Finn touched the studding, more like caressed it. This was his house and she had the sweet scent of fresh-cut lumber.

"I see the windows are cut out as I requested. I'm sure my pops and Wolfe, that's Georgie's dad, won't have any trouble installing them. Unlike me, they are master carpenters."

"Yes, but we covered them on the outside in case you hit a rainstorm on the trip back and so there won't be a drag while you are hauling her."

"Before we leave I want your suggestions on all the finishing materials, and I would really appreciate your taking time to talk to Pops. He has the list of materials you sent to me, but he'll have questions … such as the best wood for the siding."

"Not a problem. We usually install wood siding, like cedar clapboard, but there are other choices depending how you're going to finish your home. Board and batten, if you want to paint it, works well. Our tiny houses are certified RV's and are street-legal—width and height—as I told you on the phone."

"Great. Any problem with the license and insurance? Are we all set to pull her out tomorrow?"

"All completed, along with the title that you signed online."

"Georgie, look at the loft. See the cutout for the loft's skylight?"

"I see. I see. Way cool."

Cameron grinned and continued explaining the interior. "The loft is eight feet long. I think that will handle you, Finn. Six-foot-eight in width. Turn around and you'll see a second loft, two and a half feet deep—more storage or a nice display shelf. All is in the set of plans—what's been done so far—all the measurements, supplies, and the detailed plans to finish your home."

"As I said, you should have seen Pops and Wolfe pouring over them. Couple of kids."

"Let me show you the bathroom framing, ready for sink, toilet, and shower installation. And in the space to your right is the first-floor bedroom, or office, or playroom—approximately four plus feet by six plus feet. Big enough to flop a twin mattress … or not," Cameron said, with a chuckle.

"We really had a tough time deciding on the kitchen and great room layouts. You gave us too many choices, Cameron. But, as I emailed you, we did come to a decision."

"Yes, but you'll still be able to change it some, once you start working on her. Where are you going to park your house—the woods, the beach?"

"Next to a barn on the family farm. I'm going into the brewery business."

"Brewery? No kidding? I'd love to do that. My wife and I are home brewers. We wanted to open a craft brewery, even drafted a business plan. I'd love to hear how you're planning to start. How about dinner tonight with Carrie and me? Carrie's my wife."

Finn looked at Georgie. They both gave a shrug. Why not? "We'd like that. Nothing fancy, though," Finn said.

"I'll call Carrie. When we're done here—paperwork, tips and tricks—we can meet her at a local brewery I think you'll like. It's a few doors from your motel. Never hurts to see how others do business."

Chapter 12

———

CAMERON AND CARRIE FOSTER were sitting in a booth within eyesight of the front door as Finn and Georgie strolled in—a slight wave from Cameron, a nod in response from Finn. Introductions were made, Finn and Georgie hanging their hats with Cameron's on the hooks at the ends of the booth—three cowboys and a woman getting together for a beer.

Cameron had changed from jeans and a white T-shirt, stenciled with the tiny house logo on the back, to a navy polo shirt over khaki pants. Carrie stood up next to her husband, shaking Finn's and George's hands. Finn blinked. Carrie's light blue dress was the color of Kate's eyes.

"Georgie, what's your part in all this?" Carrie asked, flipping her long black braid to her back as she slid into the booth. She and Cameron made a striking couple. Both African Americans and both still very much in love, his hand rested on top of hers except when he was making a point. Both were warm and friendly. Finn quickly noted that Cameron was the serious one of the pair always getting to the point of the discussion.

"Georgie and I grew up together on Bradley Farm. We're like brothers," Finn said.

Georgie spoke up. "He's always dragging me into his schemes—case in point, racing here to pick up his house. What was I thinking?" Georgie said rolling his eyes.

"You have to try their stout," Cameron said, to Finn. "Georgie, what do you like best? Ale, Pilsner—"

"Let's just say I like an ice cold whatever. Finn hasn't educated me in the finer points of the brewery business … yet."

"A stout is a little strong for me, but you guys go ahead," Carrie said. "I'm starved, honey. Order me a burger and, Finn, you have to try the soft pretzels with salt. They are to die for."

As the orders were taken, Finn and Georgie glanced around the bar. It was packed. Large screen televisions mounted high on three walls. A panoramic view of the brewery was behind glass across the entire fourth wall.

Neon tubes of various colors were embedded in the shiny concrete bar and over the line of tap handles behind. Pendant lights hung over the island centered behind the semi-circular bar. The group of fans in front of one TV cheered as their team executed a trick play, followed by moans at another play and a missed opportunity. Whatever the action, all mixed to the beat of the latest pop music piped in overhead.

The aroma of freshly baked, salted pretzels filled the air. Burgers with fries, pretzels and a pitcher of Carrie's favorite beer, a light ale, were set on the table. Carrie poured the first round and lifted her glass. Everyone raised their glass to each other, Finn with a glass of stout.

Washing a bite of burger down with beer, Cameron turned to Finn. "Getting the permits and licenses for a brewery are brutal. Can take months, sometimes more than a year. You've probably already started the process."

Finn picked up a pretzel. "Months? A year? I had no idea."

"How many barrels a month do you figure to brew? Are you going to have a bar out front of the fermentation tanks, a tasting room to draw in the townies?"

"Definitely a bar. I like to get my guitar out at times. Folks, especially the bikers, really get into it. You should see them … set the tables back … line dance, all kinds of action."

"Are you going to offer crowlers and growlers?" Carrie asked.

Finn's eyes darted around the table. "I haven't planned that out yet, Carrie."

"A farm. Gee whiz, can you grow your own grains? Your own hops? That would be a draw—local brew from local products. How big is your farm?"

Georgie's eyes ping-ponged between the two men. Cameron was talking his language. Crops!

"She's huge. Been in the family since the mid 1800's. Pops said the big barn, the one I want to establish the brewery in, was built around 1915. The farm was thriving—a period when it was a dairy and they needed space to store feed, thrashers, tractors. It's the biggest barn on the property, bigger than the horse barn. Sits by the road, a flat area, perfect for customer parking … in the future. Trees to the side. A beautiful spot. I've been doing a little, very small scale, brewing a few bottles in the back of a tavern down the road. I'm the bartender—love the folks, their stories, strumming my guitar, entertaining everyone a bit. You should see when I put on my rhinestone cowboy shirt and pants. Big belt buckle crusted with rhinestones and the band on my hat too. Really a good time."

"Finn, I'm beat. I think it's time we say goodnight to the Fosters. We have a big day ahead," Georgie said.

"You're right. Sorry, Cameron … Carrie. I'll see you tomorrow, Cameron."

"I look forward to checking out your house with you, Finn. Have a good night," Cameron said.

"If I don't see you before you boys leave, have a safe trip home," Carrie added.

Georgie headed for the door, Finn following behind. Finn was in a daze and it wasn't from the beer. The list of what had to be done to start a brewery that Cameron had ticked off, Finn hadn't done any of them. He hadn't thought about any of them.

"Hey, mister, how about a smoke. It's the best cannabis you can get around here."

"Sure, sure. How much?"

"On the house. Stop at my shop tomorrow, if you like … just down the street. Here, try this chaw. Remember, just down the street. Al's Smoker."

Finn rarely smoked, but at the moment it seemed like a good idea. Leaving the bar he lit up and began to amble down the street. Georgie was ahead of him, already stepping in the door to their room.

———

AT HOME, GETTING READY for bed, Carrie scrutinized her husband. "What's the matter, Cam?"

"It's Finn."

"His barn raiser?"

"He's a great guy, an engaging personality, and he's doing what you and I have wanted to do, dreamed of doing."

"A brewery?"

"A brewery," Cameron sighed. "Only we talk and he's doing."

"From what you've described of his truck, I'm worried it won't make it all the way to New Hampshire," Carrie said, switching off the light.

"I know, but he loves that truck. What I like about Finn is his passion. I'll call, check in with Finn along the way, make sure he gets home safe. In the meantime, it's going to be a big day for him in the shop," Cameron said, curling around his wife.

Chapter 13

A ROOSTER'S EARLY MORNING cackle resonated from the back of the motel, drifting in the open window. Their eyes closed, both Finn and Georgie smiled. *Rise and shine. Just like home.*

"Georgie, you awake?" Finn whispered, his voice raspy, pulling the sheet over his head.

"How did Sir Winston get here? Was he hiding in the back of the truck?" Georgie whispered back.

"I like the feel of home," Finn said, yanking the sheet down.

"Speaking of feeling, how's your head. That was a pretty nasty time you spent over the john last night."

"Head's not great. Could be worse. Remind me never to accept a cigarette from a stranger again, will ya?"

"You might have guessed it was marijuana. The smoke was one thing, but the chaw sent your stomach over the edge. Let's get some coffee," Georgie said rolling his legs off the bed. "I have some aspirin in my kit. Or will that make your stomach kick up again?"

"I'll give it a try. Georgie, before I forget, Pops had a few suggestions when I called him last night ... after the head in the toilet bowl event."

"Finn, it must have been after midnight—"

"I wasn't thinking, but Pops knew what I was calling about. He suggested we buy the appliances that fit the house rather than try to get them later. He had made a few calls. He was worried I'd end up buying them from Cameron anyway, and then I'd have to pay for shipping. Also, he wants me to include the sewer stuff—the RV toilet, undercarriage tank … and, oh the shower stall, and the under-the-counter refrigerator with the freezer compartment."

"Geez, that's quite a list," Georgie said, scrubbing his scalp with his knuckles.

"He and Mom must have put their heads together and came up with the stuff so we'll be sure everything fits. They agreed I should put it on the line of credit I established at the bank for the house. No problem with finding the siding and windows in Lakeville … Portsmouth, if we have to go there. So, it's good that the rooster got us up. Lots to do today … first off, show Pop's list to Cameron. Hope he can fill the order before we leave. Oh and I'm supposed to ask Cameron if there are special sizes for the plumbing or is everything a standard size? Anything non-standard we should put on the list. My goal is to have the house built by September."

"What's special about September?" Georgie asked, heading to the bathroom for a shower.

"Nothing. But the tavern gets busy—"

"I suppose Cameron can secure the appliances by tying them to the studding inside. It may mean we can't leave today," Georgie called out.

"I know. But if they have the items in stock, then we still may be able to roll out early tomorrow morning."

"Shower's all yours, bro," Georgie said, emerging with a green bath towel tied around his waist.

"You should have taken my phone from me last night. After I called Pops, I called Kate. I was going to text her but hit the wrong button."

"Oh, oh. I must have fallen asleep. Was she mad?"

"I don't think so, but, of course, I wasn't *thinking*. Pops told me the whole family will be at the farm when we get home … even Sadie is flying up from Washington. Wolfe's already scraped down the grill—Mom wants to have a barbeque the day after we get back. I couldn't stop myself … had to ask Kate to join us."

"Did she accept your invite?"

"I think so … the line dropped, or I accidentally hit the disconnect button."

Chapter 14

———

TOWEL DRYING DAISY'S LONG blonde hair, Kate smiled at the six-year old scrunching her eyes shut.

"Do you like your new shampoo? You smell like sweet strawberries."

"Umm, I love it."

"Do you want curls or braids today, Daisy?" Kate asked, switching on the hairdryer.

"Braids, Aunt Kate. It's going to be hot today."

"Braids it is. Let's sit up on the bed. I have something to tell you while I fix your hair."

"What is it?"

With bare feet, night shirts over blue pajama bottoms, they settled on the king-sized bed. Kate brushed the little girl's hair, parting it down the back.

"I've told you about a man I work with. His name is Finn Bradley, and he's invited me to a homecoming." Kate laughed. "Daisy, he's literally hauling a tiny house on the back of his truck all the way from Colorado to New Hampshire. You've heard of Colorado?"

"I think so. It's near Wisconsin?"

"Not really. It's southwest of Wisconsin. Anyway, I think it's time you meet him. It will be like a party."

"Can Mrs. Peters come too?"

"I don't think so. But maybe she can come another time. I'm glad you like her. She's a very dependable sitter."

"She's okay, I guess. I help her clean the house and she takes me for ice cream."

"We haven't been to a party for a long time. Mr. Bradley lives on a farm and he has lots of family—brothers and sisters."

"Sounds fun. Will there be ice cream and cake?"

"I don't know. I thought I'd make some special jam, or maybe my favorite red-cabbage chutney as a gift. Want to help me?"

"Yes, Aunt Kate. I love to help you cook. Will Mrs. Peters let us use her kitchen?"

"I'm sure she will. But, Daisy, if we go to the party, we have to play a game."

"What kind of game? Hide and seek?"

Kate laughed. "Not exactly. We're going to play like you're my daughter and I'm your mother. In this game, if someone asks you about your daddy, you say you never met him. He left us before you were born. Do you think you can do that ... call me mommy?"

Daisy turned around to face Kate, her eyes intent on her aunt.

"You can't forget. No slip ups," Kate said, shaking her head.

"If I forget, does that mean we might have to move again?"

"It might. So what do you think? It's a very grown-up thing I'm asking you to do. Actually, we're living like mother and daughter anyway."

"I won't forget ... Mommy."

"That's my girl."

"I think I'll be a movie star when I grow up. Play lots of parts," Daisy said grinning.

Chapter 15

Big Red starts journey back to NH

THE DAY HAD ARRIVED—show time—Big Red pulling the house away from its nest.

The dark motel room gave way to gray, a sunbeam dashing along the worn green carpet.

In tandem, Finn's feet hit the floor as did Georgie's.

"Rock, paper, scissors," Finn said.

"For what?" Georgie replied, scrubbing his head with his fingertips.

"Who gets to drive first."

"It's going to be scary, Finn. I don't think a game is in order."

"Well, how else are we going to decide who gets the honor?"

"It's your house. You drive."

"Oh, no. That's too easy."

"Okay, but if I win, no backseat driving."

"Right."

They faced off—feet on the floor, bums on the beds.

Staring each other in the eyes—right fist hitting the palm of the left hand.

"Rock, paper, scissors," Finn called out.

Finn picked scissors.

Georgie picked paper.

"Two out of three?" Finn asked.

"Not on your life, bro. Your house. You won. You drive."

The pair showered, grabbed a coffee, and six egg McMuffins to go. It was going to be a long morning. Cameron was waiting for them, standing out in the builder's parking lot. The green tiny house twinkling in the sunlight was ready to roll to its new home.

Cameron had spent the previous day making numerous calls to local suppliers. If he wasn't successful in finding what Finn ordered, he swapped appliances with other customer's houses that weren't scheduled for immediate delivery in order to complete Finn's add-on requests. Cameron had camped out with the purchasing manager, and by the end of the day he had loaded the appliances, securing them in place for the trip to New Hampshire.

"Finn, I put together a folder with some of the stuff I saved for a brewery. There's a catalog of equipment and supplies. Toss it, if you already have the info."

"Thanks, Cameron," Finn said, tucking the folder under his arm. "I'll be talking to you. I'm sure there will be questions … about finishing my house."

Finn shook Cameron's hand. "Thanks again … for everything."

"Good luck on your trip. Let me know if I can help … whatever you need," Cameron called out, as Finn climbed behind the wheel of Big Red.

Finn backed up to the trailer hitch, Cameron on one side, Georgie the other waving Finn to the exact spot. Two more staffers hustled out of the factory and within minutes Finn's green baby was hitched, dwarfing the mighty Big Red.

"I think I can. I think I can," Finn whispered to himself. He was scared, but his nerves were trumped by excitement of the adventure ahead.

Finn's foot rested lightly on the gas pedal as Georgie hopped up in the passenger seat. Shifting into gear, the truck slowly inched out of the parking lot, turning onto the street. Finn held his breath at the sight of the green monster in his rearview mirror, but miraculously it followed him down the street leaving the builders waving, hollering goodbye and good luck.

"Hey, pretty good, Georgie?"

"Dang right, bro. Bradley Farm here we come. A little coffee to celebrate?"

"Yup. Open the spigot for me, please. I don't dare take my hands off the wheel, but I think I can manage a teeny weenie sip from the cup," Finn said, with a chuckle that crackled in his throat.

Clicking off the first hour, the boys relaxed seeing two signs, "Leaving Colorado," then a few yards later, "Welcome to Kansas."

"How we doing on gas?" Georgie asked, looking out the window at the passing farmland.

"Pretty good," Finn answered, glancing at the fuel gauge.

Suddenly the engine sputtered, the truck slowing to a stop. Both men popped out, raised the hood to find a broken fan belt. Looking at each other, their eyes swept over the miles and miles of empty plains.

"There's something up ahead, but I can't tell if it's a house, or, please, God, a gas station. Maybe a repair shop," Georgie said, holding his hand up to shade his eyes.

"Well, let's see if 9-1-1 works."

The connection made, Finn laughed at the operator questioning their location. He gave her the highway and the number of miles they had traveled east from the Colorado state line. "You can't miss us. Tell the tow truck driver to look for a big green box on the back of a red truck."

Now, all they could do was wait. Leaning against the truck, they finished the coffee, the last bite of muffin, continuing to cool their heels.

Finn checked his watch. Almost an hour had passed.

"Maybe you should call again," Georgie said. "It's getting hot out here."

"I agree." Finn punched the numbers again. He was told to be patient. The tow truck is on the way.

"Any minute," Finn said, disconnecting the call, pulling his hat lower to shade his face.

It was too hot to sit in the truck, so they sat on the road, on the shady side of the tiny house.

Finn's mind wandered seeing the pavement ripple in the heat. Was that a mirage or was something coming down the road? I wonder what Kate's doing? Tavern should be busy by now … maybe not. I wish she was here. Damn, I miss her. I wonder if she misses me. She says she does. She'd fit nicely up in the loft …

"Hear that?" Finn said, shaking loose Kate's image.

"Sure do. Maybe we'll be saved from frying to death out here," Georgie said, squinting at a truck off in the distance.

A mid-sized tow truck slowed to a stop in front of Big Red. The driver climbed out of his rig and started to laugh at the pair of eager faces looking at their savior. "You boys are in luck. There's a gas station a couple of miles ahead. Let's get that green thing off your truck—"

"Oh, no you don't. If that gas station is just down the road, then you hitch my truck to yours. We don't have to go fast, but the green thing stays where she is."

"ALRIGHT, ALRIGHT, calm down. Let's do it. We don't have time to yakity-yak. Maybe you boys haven't heard. There's a storm coming."

Finn glanced over his shoulder at the thickening clouds to the west. The tow driver, with the help of Finn and Georgie, hooked the two trucks together. Finn and Georgie jumped in Big Red as the tow driver gave his engine some fuel. At first Finn didn't think the tow truck could haul such a big load, but then Big Red jerked as the tow engaged and began rolling down the road cutting through the vast plains of wheat and barley.

The tow driver eased his load alongside the gas station such as it was. An old codger, frayed floppy hat covering his long gray hair, leaned his chair back against the convenience store, out of the sun. He rose slowly ambling toward the tow truck as Finn and Georgie hustled up to him.

"We need a fan belt. Can you help us?" Finn asked.

"Depends on the size."

"Well, do you or don't you have a fan belt," Georgie asked.

Finn shot a glare at Georgie. The heat was getting to him. "My truck's size. Come and take a look."

The tow driver unhitched his load then joined the men looking under Big Red's white snout.

"No, can't say as I have that size," the old man said, chewing on a piece of straw.

"Can you get one?" Finn asked, pushing his hat up his forehead.

"Yup. Not today. Maybe tomorrow."

The tow driver checked the broken belt. "I can get one to you tomorrow morning … not me, but the outfit I work for."

Finn sighed. Looked at Georgie. "Looks like we're spending the night out on the Kansas plains."

"I'll arrange to get it to you as soon as possible," the tow driver cut in. "Your belt is a standard size. Understand, you have to pay for it in advance … a delivery out this far."

"Thanks," Finn said, handing the tow driver his credit card. "Ask whoever has the belt to bring a couple … just in case. I'll write my cell on that bill. Call when we can expect to see the repairman. We'll be right here … can't go anywhere."

The tow truck hit the road. Georgie sighed as he turned to the station attendant. "Do you have any food in your store?"

"A little of this. A little of that. Better than nothing, I guess."

Chapter 16

Lucas

BY 9:30 THE NEXT morning Big Red was again rolling down the highway. Both Finn and Georgie were stiff from sleeping in the bed of the truck although they had thought to bring a couple of pillows and blankets when they left the farm. A scruffy repairman had arrived as promised, pawing at his beard. Georgie took one look at the guy and grabbed the two fan belts from the man's hand dangling at his side. With his experience at keeping the farm equipment running, Georgie installed the belt in short order.

The storm clouds had veered to the north leaving only a few lingering gray puffs overhead.

Passing through St. Louis, and with Indiana only a few more hours ahead, the pair relaxed. They were beginning to make up some of the time they lost from the breakdown delay. Again clicking off miles of farmland, Finn took his foot off the gas pedal.

Georgie, his head resting on a pillow against the truck's window felt the truck slow, then a jolt, as it came to a complete stop. His body jerked up. "What's the matter? Why did you stop? Not the belt again—"

"Nothing's wrong. I saw something beside the road. Looked like a puppy."

"Finn, this is no time to pick up a dog."

"Can't hurt to look can it?"

Finn clamored out of the truck, jogged several yards back down the road. A puppy sat off to the side. His head cocked, the pup's big brown eyes melted Finn's heart. Kneeling by the little guy, he felt for a collar under the red neckerchief tied around the pup's neck. The dog's curly, biscuit-colored fur was dirty, his paws caked with mud. His tail tentatively swiped over the road's dirt shoulder.

"Hey, little guy. You okay? There, there, don't shake. I won't hurt you."

Georgie sauntered up. With his arms crossed over his chest he peered down at the mutt. It was obvious the puppy was going to join the adventure.

Finn picked up the little dog, tucked him under his arm petting his head. The pup's muzzle reached up, giving Finn's cheek a lick. "See there, he likes us, Georgie. Someone must have dumped him from the looks of his fur, his paws. Let's give him a drink of water then you drive."

Georgie shook his head. No point arguing. Once Finn's heart was touched, there was no way to change his mind. "I'll dump the dregs of my coffee. His nose is small enough he'll be able to drink out of the cup."

Setting the dog in the bed of the truck, Finn poured a little of his bottled water in Georgie's foam cup, a few specs of coffee grounds clinging to the inside. "No collar. What should we name him?"

"Well, he's a little hobo ... how about Hobo?" Georgie said.

"No, no, he's a survivor. You know those pictures of the dogs playing poker? I swear this little guy looks like one of them ... Cool

Hand Luke?" Finn said, stashing the empty cup in the crate of tools tucked against the back of the truck's bed.

"Too long," Georgie said, climbing up behind the wheel.

Finn slid up onto the passenger's seat, pulling his shirt over the dog's little body. "Luke? Lucas! That's it. Well, Lucas? Do you like your new name?"

The pup squirmed his head out of the shirt's cocoon, letting out a whine in agreement.

"See there, Georgie? He agrees. Lucas it is. I know a pretty lady who is going to love you," Finn said.

Georgie rolled his eyes, checking the rearview mirror as he pulled Big Red back onto the road. "Holy cow, Finn, the clouds are really black and they're coming on us fast."

Finn squinted at the side view mirror. "Wow. You're right. Looks bad. Up ahead ... up ahead ... that overpass. Step on it. We'll wait it out. Should be enough room for us to pull through ... I think."

"I think so too. We haven't had any trouble with other overpasses. I'll pull under far enough ... so the house is under the road."

Both men quickly rolled up their windows as debris hit the side of the truck. Lucas burrowed deep under Finn's shirt.

"Almost there. Give her more gas, Georgie. Hurry. Hurry. Crap. It's dark out. Hurry."

"She's full out ... have to slow or we'll squirt out the other side."

"And. What was that?" Finn asked.

"Thunder ... I think. Now, we're under. Can you tell if the house is shielded?"

"I can't tell and I don't think we should get out. Hunker down in your seat, Georgie. Turn the engine off," Finn said, his voice loud in his ears.

"It is off. That roar is outside ... over us. Finn, I think a tornado is going right over us. Do you think it'll rip off the overpass?"

"I don't know … no … look … it's up ahead … went right over us. Georgie, I can't look. Is the house still there?"

Georgie opened his door.

"No, no, don't get out," Finn said, grabbing Georgie's arm.

"It's gone, Finn."

"What do you mean? My house is gone?"

"No, the tornado, stupid." Georgie walked around the house, returned to his seat behind the wheel. "She's okay, Finn. Raining buckets. Let's sit here until it stops."

"Whew. Good idea."

Suddenly hazy light from the setting sun replaced the thick black clouds.

"You don't think we'll catch up to those clouds do you?" Finn asked as Georgie turned the engine over, easing the load out from under the highway above.

"I don't think Big Red is up for speeding."

Lucas poked his head out. "Lucas and I are hungry, aren't we boy?"

"Me too. A burger and a beer would be good. I don't mind telling you, Finn. That was scary."

Finn slouched back in his seat releasing some of the tension that gripped his body. "After we grab something to eat, let's stop for the night. Rest up."

Chapter 17

———

THE CALM AFTER THE storm softened to twilight as Indiana welcomed Big Red hauling the tiny house clothed in green zipboard.

"Where's a diner when you want one," Finn said, watching out the windshield for a restaurant as they approached the outskirts of a small town.

"I bet we'll find a spot here. How about that bar up ahead. Harry's Bar and Grille. Sounds just like what we're looking for," Georgie said, leaning forward against the steering wheel.

"No matter. Let's stop. I'm so hungry I could eat a possum."

"Really?"

"Figure of speech. We'll leave Lucas in the cab."

The pup put his paws on the edge of the window, nose up sniffing the breeze. Turning to Finn, his furry muzzle let out a whine.

"Don't you worry, little guy. You'll have your own burger."

Georgie eased the truck with its trailer into Harry's parking lot and stopped. Hopping out of the cab, he performed a couple touch-your-toes pulling the kinks out of his back.

Finn joined him, rolling the windows down a crack for Lucas and then locking the truck.

The pair strolled into Harry's which was almost as dark as outside. Walking to the bar, they hitched up on the stools, each ordering a beer from the bartender. Finn shot a glance at Georgie.

Did he notice the tattoos covering the burly bartender's exposed upper-body parts—arms to shoulders, and around his neck.

"I'll have a couple burgers, some fries to go with the beer," Finn said. "Same for my friend here."

A group of bikers sitting at a table behind Finn and Georgie made a remark about the new hayseeds. They were joined by two more bikers who sauntered into the bar. "You should see the itty bitty house outside. The two at the bar drove her in. So sweet," he said, in a falsetto, puckering his lips, followed with a few kissy sounds in the air.

"Sweet? Well, maybe they're sweeties ... like sweet on each other." The big talker walked up, his shoulder grazing Georgie's shoulder. "How about it? You sweet on your friend here?"

"Knock it off. Go sit with your buddies," Georgie said, shoving the guy back.

"Hey, Billie, you see that. Cutie pie has his tutu in a bunch."

"I said, get lost," Georgie said, sliding off the stool. He gave the guy another shove on the shoulder, then another shove on his chest."

"I don't think so, sweetie," the smarty mouth hissed, hauling off a punch in Georgie's face which brought Finn to his feet. No one was going to punch Georgie and remain standing.

The other bikers joined the melee as three off-duty officers strolled in for a cold one after their shift. The cops mixed it up with the bikers, trying to break them apart not noticing that two men hightailed it out of the bar, clamoring into the beat-up red truck hauling a green monster. The pair made a fast getaway out of the parking lot and down the road. Lucas ducked under Finn's shirt to keep from falling on the floor. Around a bend a big sign appeared on the roadside: *You are Leaving Indiana. Welcome to Ohio.*

"That was close, bro," Georgie said. "I'm sorry ... lost my head. I wasn't going to let those guys get away trying to bully us."

"Don't be sorry. That creep deserved more than we gave him. Are you okay? Your face doesn't look so good." Finn said.

"Me? What about you? Don't look in the mirror … you'll scare yourself," Georgie said, with a chuckle. "Open that pack of wipes under your seat. Be careful. Don't squash Lucas when you bend over."

"Really? How do I look?"

"Like you've been in a fight. I can't tell if you won or lost," Georgie said.

"Well, as I recall, we whipped their asses good," Finn said, grinning.

Five miles down the road, Georgie pulled into a McDonalds. The pair took turns in the restroom, washing blood off their faces from cut lips and swollen eyes. Georgie went back to the truck and waited while Finn loaded up with sacks of burgers, fries, milkshakes, and a soup bowl to put a burger in for Lucas.

He set the sacks down on a table by the door, pulled out his cell, and tapped Kate's number.

———

"HI, KATIE, IT'S ME, FINN."

"I know it's you, silly. How is everything going?"

"Not too bad. Georgie and I make a good team. Katie—"

"Yes, I'm here."

"I had this dream. I came home and you were gone. I don't want you to leave."

"I'm still here. Your sister, Jeli, stopped by the tavern. Introduced herself. That's some fiery red hair she has."

"Did she have something special on her mind?"

"No. Probably just being friendly. That scary guy came in last night."

"Scarface?" Finn asked.

"Uh huh. Louie stayed in the back. Scarface just kept twirling a coin on the counter. Didn't say anything. Had a beer and left."

"You, okay?"

"I am, but I'll be glad when you get back. When do you think?"

"If all goes well. No more fights—"

"Fights?"

"Ah, nothing much. A little skirmish. We gave as good as we got, but Georgie's got a nasty black eye."

"Are you all right?"

"Hunky-dory. I'm planning on stopping by Louie's on the way to the farm so you and Louie can see my house. Maybe tomorrow afternoon. I'll let you know. Well, gotta go. Georgie's waving at me. Night, Katie."

"Night, Finn."

Chapter 18

———

MOIST WARM AIR FLOATED in the truck's open windows. In spite of the fresh air, Georgie was fidgety, trying to find a comfortable angle, his head on a pillow scrunched up to soften the edge of the window casing. At each twist, Lucas snuggled deeper in his lap. It didn't seem to matter to the pup who was sitting in the passenger seat. A lap was a lap.

Big Red's headlights flashed on the large billboard as it passed—Truck stop ahead 5 miles. Finn was dead tired and he knew Georgie was too. It was 11:35. They had to stop, had to catch some ZZZs in back of the truck. They could take advantage of the truck stop's showers, eat a good breakfast, and be back on the road before sunrise. With any luck they would be home around mid-day.

Kate's image popped into Finn's head. Actually, it never left. She's so pretty. I'll give her a hug, a big hug, even a kiss, he thought. Maybe I'm just fantasizing, being away from her for so many days. If she hugs me back then I'll definitely kiss her. What was that word Jeli used to describe Sadie … oh, that's it. Sadie was besotted with Travis. He looked it up. The definition described how he felt perfectly—intoxicated, infatuated. Yep, all of that.

Georgie's eyelids raised as Finn parked under the floodlights along with an RV, and two oil tankers. "What's up?" he murmured, Lucas's tail thumping against his ribs.

Finn glanced at him, patted the pup's head. "Do you want to eat first, shower first, or sleep first?"

"Where are we?"

"I figure we have a shot to be home tomorrow afternoon. But I can't drive another mile," Finn said, yawning.

"I'm with you but I'm hungry. Let's shower, grab a steak sandwich and eat in the back with Lucas."

"You get your shower while I take Lucas over to those bushes. Then you get our sandwiches while I shower. Lucas will be okay in the truck," Finn said.

"Sounds like a plan, bro. Except I'm so stiff I'm not sure I can stand up. Take a look at my right eye when you get out will ya? I think it's swollen shut."

Finn snapped the new leash on the pup's new collar he picked up at a Dollar Store across from the last gas station. He swung out of the truck, stretched his back up straight as Lucas jumped down. Georgie walked around so Finn could take a look at his eye. "Hmmm, your eye is turning an ugly yellowish purple, but you're standing in the shadows of the floodlights. How does it feel?"

"Fine, unless I touch it. Thanks again for your help last night … at the bar. Not sure how it all happened. Tired I guess, or the tutu remark. Stupid. Not sure what Dad's going to say," Georgie said, kicking an empty soda can.

"Don't worry about Wolfe. Now, Jeli will be a different matter. She'll probably tease us to death," Finn said with a chuckle. "Go get your shower, and it wouldn't hurt to try a little soap and water on that face."

"You too, Finn. You have a cut over your eye."

"Stopped bleeding didn't it?"

"I can't tell. But blood's not running down your cheeks, if that's what you're asking. How are you? You seem a little … I don't know, a little down?"

"I'm fine … mulling over stuff. Go get your shower."

Georgie grabbed his duffel bag from behind the seat and took off in the direction of the showers.

Lucas did his business under a bush then trotted happily back to the green thing with his master. Leaning against the back wall of his house, Finn pulled out his cell.

"Hi, Pops, it's me, your very, very tired son. Sorry for the late call. Did I wake you?"

"No. Your mom and I were just lying in bed. Everyone is here at the farm. Where are you guys. When can we expect you?"

"Georgie and I think we'll make it sometime tomorrow. No later than mid afternoon, unless we have some kind of trouble."

Lucas tugged on the leash barking at a white poodle behind the window of the RV next to the green thing.

"Is that a dog barking?"

"Yes sir. We'll have lots of stories. See you tomorrow. I'll call when we're within a couple hours." Finn disconnected the call and immediately tapped number one on his speed dial.

"Hi, Finn. Are you almost home?"

"Hi, baby. It's good to hear your sweet voice … you sound sleepy. I woke you didn't I? I'm sorry—"

"Maybe … it's okay."

"We're almost home—tomorrow, two, three, fourish. I can't wait to see you. Don't be surprised if I give you a big old bear hug, if that's okay with you?" It was the first time he called her baby. It slipped out.

Kate giggled. "Of course, that's okay with me, silly. I can't wait to see the house."

"Don't forget, dinner at the farm the next day. Tell Louie I suggested he close the tavern. He's invited too. He can borrow my Harley—it's stored in his shed. He has the key. But I'll pick you up. Geez, you already know about my motorcycle. Sorry. Georgie and I are dead tired."

Finn paused, running the toe of his sneaker over a crack in the pavement. "Katie?"

"I'm here."

"I miss you. I mean … I really miss you."

Chapter 19

⸻

HIS HEART RACING, palpitating against the walls of his chest, Finn turned into the parking lot of the Cock & Feathers Tavern. Climbing out of Big Red, a smile spread across his face. There she was, popping out of the tavern's back door, running to him, the ties of her apron flying out behind her. Suddenly she paused, hesitating, but Finn didn't hesitate. He strode to her, wrapped his arms around her, and laid a searing hot kiss on her eager lips.

Swinging her in the air, they both laughed, her arms reaching around his neck. Setting her on her feet, but still holding her tight, Finn whispered in her ear. "I've missed you more than you'll ever know, Katie girl."

"Ah-huh." Georgie tapped Finn on the shoulder.

Finn reluctantly dropped one arm but kept the other in a grip around Kate's waist. "Kate, this is Georgie. Georgie meet Kate."

"Nice to finally meet you, Kate."

"Same here. Finn talks about you all the time."

"Not as much as he talks about you, I'll bet."

Kate stepped to Georgie, giving him a brief hug. "Hey, that eye doesn't look good." She turned to Finn scanning his face. "And, that cut over your eye is just as bad. Come on you two, let me see if we can't clean up your faces or you'll scare your folks."

Kate saw nothing except Finn when he got out of the truck, but suddenly she was aware of the green monster attached to it. "Wow! I mean … a really big WOW! How did you ever make it home? No way your truck could pull that huge crate over two thousand miles."

"We broke down once, but we babied her along. She never exactly raced down the road," Finn said with his proud-papa smile. "She did a heck of a job."

They were interrupted when a light-tan ball of fur raced up to Finn, jumping up and down on his cowboy boots.

"And who is this little fella?" Kate asked, scooping up the puppy, cooing how pretty he is, petting his silky head as he licked her fingers.

"He's a little hobo. Found him on the side of the road. His name is Lucas," Finn said, a perpetual grin on his face.

"How appropriate. Yes, Lucas, you're a good boy ... and if I'm right you're a Lucas Terrier."

"Does that mean he's going to be big as a papa bear?" Georgie asked.

"That means he's a tiny version of papa bear. Probably twenty pounds max. A friend of mine had one. So cute," Kate said, setting the pup on the ground. Finn held the back door open for her, as she snapped her fingers for Lucas to follow. "Come on, Lucas, you too. I'll get you a bowl of water."

Finn smirked at Georgie. *That's my girl.*

"As I was saying, Kate, it's good to see you. Finn's been mooning around since the minute we pulled out of the builder's lot."

"Hey, what's going on back here?" Louie said, hustling in from the grill to welcome his bartender home. Sticking out his hand, Finn gave it a hearty shake. "That's quite a rig you have out there, Finn. Miracle you made it back ... ah ... not exactly in one piece, I see." Louie looked from Finn to Georgie. "You boys got mixed up in a brawl, did ya?"

"You might say that, Louie," Georgie said laughing. "But we escaped. Far as we know, they're still punching each other."

"Hey, Louie, did Kate tell you there's going to be a homecoming celebration at the farm? Well, it's an early dinner tomorrow afternoon. Can you make it? The tavern—"

"Wouldn't miss it, and yes, Kate mentioned it. That's Monday, so we're not too busy anyway. Your fill-in can hold the fort down for a few hours. And, I want to see the inside of that green tank."

"Great, you ride the Harley and I'll pick up Kate—"

"No need for the Harley. I'll drive my car. Now, I have to get back out front. Someone has to tend to the customers," Louie said with a grin. "Good to have you back, son."

"I'll be with you in a minute, Louie," Kate said, over her shoulder. "I want to clean these wicked wounds on the guys' faces. Okay, you two. Sit down on that crate of potatoes."

Kate dabbed soap and water around Georgie's eye. The swelling had gone down and the yellowish purple had turned to a dim grayish yellow.

"Thanks, Kate. I'll take Lucas for a walk while you cleanup, Finn. Take your time," Georgie said, as he pushed the door open, clucking at Lucas to follow.

"I have something—"

Both Kate and Finn spoke at once.

"You go first," Finn said, his eyes narrowing, brows drawn together. He wasn't smiling, but he noticed Kate wasn't smiling either.

"No, no, you go ahead," Kate said, setting the washcloth on the edge of the sink.

Finn sat her down on a crate of empty bottles, pulling another up beside her. "Rock, paper, scissors."

"Really, Finn, this is serious—"

He didn't crack a smile, wagging his fingers at her like a pair of scissors.

"Okay, okay. Ready?" Kate said.

Finn nodded hitting the palm of his left hand with his right fist. He came up with scissors and she with an open palm—paper.

"You first, Kate. You look serious. Whatever you want to tell me, it can't be that bad."

"It is … may change everything … between us."

"Go on."

"Tomorrow, the farm, meeting your family."

"Yesss."

"I'm … I'm bringing my daughter, Daisy."

Finn's brows shot up. "I thought you said you weren't married."

"I'm not … wasn't. Daisy's father left us … before she was born."

"How old is Daisy?"

"Six. She's very sweet. The lady … where we live … takes care of her while I'm working. I pay her." Kate looked down, her hands clasped together to stop the shaking.

"I thought she was a friend."

"A friend of a friend," Kate said.

"Hey, it's okay, Katie," Finn lifted her chin so he could look into her eyes. "A single mom is a hard job. I'm proud of you … and I'm looking forward to meeting Daisy. Pops and Mom will be delighted to have a little person around. None of us have given them a grandchild, so believe me, meeting Daisy will mean an even bigger celebration. I'll pick you and Daisy up. You hear?"

"I hear." Kate smiled through the tears rolling down her cheeks.

Finn reached for the wet cloth, dabbing her tears away. "Are you okay getting home on the Harley today? If not I'll—"

"I'll be fine. The Harley worked fine. I take it slow. Thanks for letting me borrow it while you were gone. Oh, Finn, I'm so glad you're home."

Finn stood drawing Kate up into his arms. "Me too."

"Okay, it's your turn. Tell me what's the matter. For such a successful trip you have a very gloomy look on your face. Where's the happy-go-lucky—"

"I can't do it, Katie. I can't start a brewery." His eyes turned sad, searching her face for understanding.

"Why do you say that? You've been making homebrew for years you said. The kegs, here—" Katie waved her hand over the two kegs.

"This is pathetic. I talked with a home brewer at the tiny house company. He was amazing. He knew so much. I know nothing."

"Don't give up, Finn. You've been dreaming of your own brewery. You've learned a lot here at Louie's. More than you realize, I'm sure." She reached for his hand, held it to her cheek. "You can do it."

Finn shook his head. "I'll pick you up tomorrow, noonish. If there's a change, I'll call you. Now, don't you worry about Daisy. Any daughter of yours will be a winner," he said sealing his words with a warm kiss. He wanted to share more about the doubts creeping in. More and more he doubted he could actually establish a brewery business. But it was so good to hold Katie, he didn't want to put a pall over their reunion.

Chapter 20

———

BRADLEY FARM WAS BECOMING a landmark for townies and tourists and now something new was afoot. Asphalt had been spread along one side and to the back of the barn, connecting the driveway to the antiques barn on the opposite side.

Georgie stuck his hand out the window slapping the side of the truck. "Would you look at that, Finn? You're practically in business. A parking lot," he said a grin spreading from ear to ear. With no response, Georgie glanced at Finn. He was all business, as he navigated up the driveway, turning onto the new asphalt. He carefully parked the trailer behind the barn to the spot where Pops had suggested. The plan was to use the backend as a workshop for the next couple of months while the men finished construction on the house.

Finn stared blindly out the windshield. His house in place, he turned the ignition key off. Big Red's engine seemed to heave a sigh of relief as it ground to a halt. She had done her job.

"Come on, buddy. The welcoming committee awaits your beaming face. Let go of whatever is bothering you … for them. Your pops and my dad have been working non-stop. Parking lot, transferring tools from the old horse barn down here—"

"I know." Finn let out a tortured sigh. "Now, it's show time. Come on Lucas. Your new family awaits."

Finn climbed out of the truck, the pup under his arm. Seeing the humans running toward him, Lucas squirmed free of Finn's grip.

Jeli led the way, racing down the driveway, locking her brother in a hug, hugging Georgie.

Wolfe was on her heels, first shaking Finn's hand, then unable to help himself, pulling him into a warm hug, patting his back. He hugged Georgie next, whispering in his son's ear, "Well done, but you look beat."

The whole clan was dressed in jeans and sneakers, topped with various colored T-shirts, except for Gran. She wore her usual housedress, this one in cotton with tiny purple flowers scattered on the fabric, and sturdy brown shoes on her feet.

Lucas couldn't contain himself, dancing around, running to the grass, peeing. Relieved, he raced back, jumping up and down barking, "Look at me."

Jeli knelt on the driveway. "And who are you, little fella?" she said, laughing at the pup trying to kiss her hand, her neck, her face, whatever was in reach.

"Finn named him Lucas. A hobo he saw abandoned on the road somewhere in Missouri," Georgie said.

"Hey, how do we see inside? Can you open the door?" Wolfe said, touching the green zipboard.

"There are cutouts for the windows. The builder covered them with the zipboard for traveling," Finn said.

Pops, holding Jane's hand, hustled up to their son. "Well done, Finn. Looks like a beauty, from what I can see anyway."

Jane caught a look in her son's eyes. Something was wrong. "You boys must be tired," she said. "Come on up to the house. Beer on tap, well, bottles anyway." There it was again, his eyes. A slight wince at something she said?

"Hey, little brother, give your big brother a hug." Marshall strode up, confidence in every stride. His twin, Sadie, was smiling holding her fiancé's hand as the pair joined Marshall. Finn caught the gesture—a couple in love. He wished he was holding Katie's hand right now.

"Finn, open the door. It's locked. Come on, you have to give us a peek," Jeli said, her mop of red curls bouncing with every step as she pointed to the front door ... the only door.

Finn pulled his key ring from his pants pocket and unlocked the dark red door.

Jeli popped in first. "Wow!"

Her exclamation brought Wolfe inside, then Pops, then Jane and Gran. With the windows covered with zipboard, the only light was from the open door behind them. Travis, his arm resting around Sadie's shoulders like she was going to fly away, her arm around his waist, decided to wait until it was clear.

Gran and Jane stepped out laughing at the small space, not sure how it was ever going to work. Finn joined the animated conversation between Pops and Wolfe admiring the studding, talking about how they had studied the floor plans, pointing out the kitchen and a closet area. They paid particular attention to the under-counter refrigerator, the three-burner stove with an oven, appliances strapped to the studding ready to be installed. "Wasn't expecting an oven," Pops said, smiling up at Finn.

"And, there's an under-the-counter washer-dryer combo," Finn added.

"No kidding. What do you say, Wolfe? Looks like fun?"

"Finn, can we tackle her in the morning?" Wolfe asked.

"You got it. In fact, Pops, how about being the foreman?"

Danny's eyes opened wide. "You mean it, son?"

"Sure I mean it."

"Janie," he called out to his wife. "Let's get dinner on the table. I have to get to bed, so I'll be fit as a fiddle in the morning. I've just been made Finn's foreman for this grasshopper."

Marshall, Sadie and Travis laughed, hearing Pops, as they stepped inside. They asked Finn to give them a guided tour so they could visualize the layout.

The tour over, Finn locked up, and strode next to Georgie up the driveway to the farmhouse, Lucas scampering as fast as his little legs could go ahead of his two masters. Gran had called out that it was time for dinner. No one dared to be late or they'd catch a surly look, meaning that chocolate cake was on the line.

Jeli and Sadie helped with the serving dishes—platters of country fried chicken, buttermilk biscuits, green beans laced with almonds and chunks of red pepper.

Danny, catching his wife wipe a tear away, put his arm around her. "What's wrong, Janie."

"Nothing's wrong, dear. Everything is just right. Beautiful. All of our children, and more. Travis ...he and Sadie." Her eyes filled with happy tears, looking up at her husband.

"Yup. It's pretty special. I love you, sweetheart," he whispered in her ear.

Lucas followed Jeli back and forth to the table. Finally he sat down and barked.

"Yes, yes, you'll get some too. Finn, do you have some dog food in the truck?"

"Yep, I'll bring it up later. Just give him some bits of biscuit in a bowl. That'll tide him over. But, no begging at the table."

"Come on, Lucas, don't you worry. His bark is worse than his bite."

Georgie walked around the table pouring the wine, a bottle of rosé and a bottle of chardonnay.

Gran took hold of Jane's hand on one side, Danny's on the other, and bowed her head. Everyone followed suit.

"Dear Lord, I can't thank you enough for the blessings of this day. My family is here and growing. So happy that Travis could join us. My love to Arnie, and oh yes, thank you for little Lucas ... I think. Amen."

The blessing said, chatter picked up slowly, building to raucous laughter as Georgie and Finn regaled the group with the first scary moments when they pulled out of the builder's driveway, then when the truck broke down and they had to spend the night on the bed of the truck, then finding the little hobo, and then the bar fight. Everyone immediately turned to Georgie, scanning his face.

"Your eyes don't look so bad," Jeli said, scrunching her brows.

"Oh, you should have seen them before Kathleen washed my face—ice on the eye, and then a little eye makeup over the yellow."

In tandem, everyone turned to Finn. Kathleen?

"Finn, who's Kathleen?" Sadie asked.

"I know," Jeli said. "She's Finn's new girlfriend, but she goes by Kate. If he stopped at the tavern before coming to the farm, I'd say she's more than a girlfriend. Come on, bro ... give," she said in a deep voice.

"Finn, you've mentioned a girl, a woman working at the tavern. Is she Kate?" Jane asked.

"Yes, everyone, she's Kate, and I've invited her and Louie to dinner tomorrow. Mom, you said tomorrow was going to be the homecoming celebration. I mean, there was no guarantee that Georgie and I would make it home today—"

"Of course, son, and Kate is more than welcome. So is Louie," Jane said.

"She's bringing her daughter, Daisy. She's six."

"Oh, oh, is there a husband?" Jeli asked.

"No. Kate's never been married. The father left her before Daisy was born. She—"

"She's brave raising her daughter alone," Gran said.

"No matter if there's a husband or not." Jane grinned at Danny. "One never is quite sure how things happen—cart before the horse or after. It was sex after our wedding when your father and I conceived Sadie and Marshall." Her face turned red at what she just divulged. "Your father left two days later for his Army post. And, there I was. Of course I didn't know I was pregnant. Gran figured it out before I did. She marched me to the doctor's office." Jane turned to Gran, patting her hand. "Then, your grandmother invited me to stay in the farmhouse ... permanently."

"Well, someone had to look after you ... with child. You were just a baby yourself."

Dinner wound down, and Jeli and Georgie began clearing the table.

"Pops, can you come with me to get Lucas his dog food?"

"Sure can, son." Danny stood up, stretched, and shook his prosthetic limb. "Just a sec, I have to wake up my leg. I've been sitting too long. Let's go, I'm ready."

Jane looked after her husband and her son, a slight smile on her lips. Maybe Finn will reveal to his father what's bothering him.

———

"THAT WAS QUITE AN adventure you had, son."

"You can say that again." Finn stuck his thumbs under his belt, as they sauntered down the driveway. "Pops, when did you know that Mom was the one? I mean, knew that you wanted to spend the rest of your life with her?"

Danny laughed. "That's the same question, exact same words, I asked my dad after I met your mother. We'd only been out on a few dates. We were still in high school, just graduating, so you can imagine I was a little afraid to ask him such a question."

"What did he say?"

"He thought a minute. He was sitting on a bale of hay next to me. He carefully selected a piece of straw and began chewing the end. Then he said, 'From the minute I saw her.' I can remember as if it was yesterday. Seems to me, son, you have a lot bouncing around in that head of yours."

Chapter 21

———

HIS DREAMS OF A brewery crushed, Finn struggled to push the black thoughts of yet another unfulfilled project from his mind. He swapped his bartender clothes for a pair of khaki slacks and a white polo shirt, leaving his hat on the bed. This was a special day, a day when his family would meet Kate. He borrowed Georgie's car making room for an extra passenger, Kate's daughter Daisy.

Breaking into a smile as he turned into the driveway where Kate lived, he slapped the wheel of the car, the black thoughts gone. He couldn't believe his eyes. Kate was standing on the grass with a little girl, a picture image of her mother. Both had blonde curls cascading around their shoulders and down their backs. The sight of Kate sent his heart pounding again. A sleeveless sundress, the fabric crossing over in front cinching at her tiny waist, floated in a kaleidoscope of blues over her slender body to just above her knees. White sandals graced her feet. The blues of the dress accentuated her blue eyes, today a deep blue crinkling in a smile at him.

The young girl, her fingers wrapped around a nosegay of wild flowers, her other hand clutched her mother's hand. She was dressed in white capris and sneakers. Her blue T-shirt matched a blue in her mother's dress.

Finn shook his head. He must be dreaming. His heart seized with love at the sight of the two golden-haired angels waiting for him.

Hopping out of the car, he walked slowly to the little girl, squatting down to her size.

"Hello, Daisy. I'm Finn," he said softly, extending his hand. "I'm so happy you're coming to dinner at Bradley Farm."

Daisy looked up at Kate, and then jutted her hand out, her blue eyes sparkling. The timid look a second before was replaced with a big smile. She trusted the man smiling at her. Finn stood up, kissed Kate's cheek, then picked up Daisy's hand. "How about I play chauffeur? You two hop in the back."

"All right, Mr. Finn. We like games. Don't we, Mommy?"

"Hold on a minute, you two. Let me take your picture, in fact I'll probably be taking your pictures all day," Finn said with a chuckle. "Say cheese … okay, in the car."

Kate nodded, letting Daisy climb in the car first, scooting over so Kate had room to sit. Kate buckled the little girl's seatbelt, along with a wide-eyed glare. *Watch yourself, little one.*

Finn backed out to the road and headed the few miles to the farm. "Have you ever been to a farm, Daisy?" he said, looking in the rearview mirror at her.

"No, sir, I haven't."

"If it's okay with your mommy, you can knock off the mister and the sir. Just call me Finn … that is if I can call you Daisy."

"Is Finn okay with you, Mommy?"

"Yes, but be respectful." That was accompanied with another glare from her *mommy.* "Finn, Louie sends his regrets. Seems your stand-in had other plans. But he expects a special tour of your house when you're ready."

Kate saw the sign for Bradley Farm before Finn made the turn. Undulating farmland broken here and there with sharp granite outcrops. "The farm's beautiful, Finn."

"Before the Bradleys, it was all forest. Then acre after acre was cleared by the first Marshall Bradley when he bought the land and built the house in 1840."

Parking at the back door of the farmhouse, Finn opened Kate's door, Daisy scooting out behind her.

The garden was in full bloom—spikes of blue, purple, pink, and white. On a rise by the horse barn, a weathered windmill swirled lazily in the afternoon sun.

Jane had prepped everyone not to rush up and scare the little girl when they arrived, but Jeli couldn't contain herself. She rushed up to Daisy, scooping her up in her arms. "You are just the prettiest little girl I've ever seen. Are you Daisy?"

Daisy giggled as Jeli set her on her feet. "Yes, ma'am," Daisy said grinning, reaching for Kate's hand.

"Hey, everyone let me introduce you to Kate and her daughter Daisy. And, everyone nod your head as I call out your name. This is another game, Daisy. We're big on games," Finn said with a wink. "First, are my mom, pops, and Gran. Come on, nod your head, Gran. Kate, you met Georgie yesterday, but this is a first for Daisy. Nod your head, Georgie. The next distinguished gentleman with the salt and pepper hair is Georgie's dad. We all call him Wolfe. Daisy, you can call him Wolfe, too, because he'd keel over if you called him Mr. Wolfe. Then meet Jeli, who twirled you around. She's the baby of the family."

Daisy giggled at the grown woman being called the baby of the family.

"Next are my big sister and brother—Sadie and Marshall. They're twins, Daisy. The man standing with his arm around my big sis, is Travis, her fiancé. Do you know what a fiancé is, Daisy?"

"Oh, yes. They're married."

"Not married quite yet. But soon."

Kate tapped Daisy on the shoulder, nodding to Finn's grandmother. Daisy nodded back and stepped tentatively to the gray-haired lady Finn introduced as Gran, holding up the flowers she had picked that morning.

"For me?" Gran said, bending over to accept Daisy's gift. "Thank you, Daisy. I think I'll put them in a vase on our dinner table."

The barking inside the back door was not letting up. Wolfe stepped to the door freeing Lucas. Racing about, the pup didn't know who to go to first. Then he saw the little girl and raced to her as fast as his little legs would go.

Daisy plopped on the ground, put her arms around the pup as he licked her face. She laughed, cooing how cute he was at which point he laid on the ground, four paws in the air, to let the little girl scratch his tummy.

Standing Daisy back on her feet, Kate looked at Finn to do something with the dog.

"Well, my new little friend," Finn said, taking her hand, "if you think Lucas is cute wait until you see the baby goats. Brother and sister. But, we'll save that until after dinner."

"Come on Daisy," Jeli said, taking over the duty of Auntie Jeli. "You and I will wash our hands and then it's dinnertime. Will you help me set the table? That's my job and I could sure use a helper the way this family is growing."

The family trooped into the house behind Jeli. Finn took Kate's hand, holding her back. "I hope this isn't too overwhelming for you? The family's been wanting children at the dinner table for a long time. So, I'm afraid Daisy is going to be loved to death."

"They're wonderful ... it's just ... it's just I hope Daisy doesn't disappoint them."

"You've got to be kidding. She's adorable and you've brought her up with loads of manners."

AFTER DINNER, HOLDING DAISY'S hand on one side and Kate's on the other, Finn gave them a quick tour of the farm, mainly pointing out the barns, and then strolling down to the goats' pen.

By the time Daisy carried one goat, and the other, to show Kate, and then rolling on the grass with Lucas, it was time to rejoin the family.

"Would you like to take a nap, Daisy, way upstairs in my bedroom?" Jeli asked.

Daisy nodded her head and Jeli looked at Kate for her sign of approval. With Kate's smile, the three trudged up the stairs.

"This is your bedroom, Jeli? It's so pretty. I'll feel like a princess," Daisy said, as Kate helped her up on the four-poster bed draped with flowers.

"We'll leave the door ajar," Jeli said as Lucas made a flying leap for the bed. Missing, he tried again, Jeli giving him a boost. Daisy's eyes were already closed.

Outside the family gathered on lawn chairs enjoying the warm air, the last days of June. The chocolate cake was polished off with coffee, tea, or milk, as they relaxed. Pops had a perpetual smile on his face. He kept glancing at the edge of the tiny house poking out from behind the barn down by the road. With his appointment as foreman, he couldn't wait to get his hands on the saws, hammers and nails. After this morning's coffee, he and Wolfe had gathered up all the plans and numerous notes, laying them out on a long table in the barn's workshop.

"Sorry to break up this celebration but we have a plane to catch," Travis said, holding out his hand to Sadie.

Marshall leaned forward in his chair. "That's my cue to polish off the coffee. I'm driving my little sis and her beau to the airport." He feigned surprise at the punch on his arm from Sadie. She was twenty minutes his senior and did not like being called *little* sis. "This sure has been fun," Marshall said grinning at Sadie. "Finn, you never cease to amaze me. That house of yours is very tiny, but cute. Clever how storage space is tucked into every nook and cranny, at least from what I saw on the building plans. I can't wait to see it finished. Of course, with a foreman like Pops in charge, I know it'll be perfect."

Getting to their feet, stretching, the hugs began as they said goodbye to each other, along with reminders of the fourth of July get-together in a little over a week.

Sadie's arms circled Kate. "I'm so glad we met. And Daisy is precious." Turning to her mom, she kissed her cheek. "Sorry, Travis and I won't be able to fly up on the Fourth. We'll miss you. Make sure we get lots of pictures. And that goes for you, too, Pops. Watch out that you hit the nail more than your fingers."

"Don't you worry about me. Travis, we're so glad you could join us," Pops said, shaking hands and then pulling his future son-in-law into a bear hug.

Travis shook hands with the rest of the men, hugging Gran and Jane in turn. They both planted a peck on his cheek, Gran brushing a tear away. "Kate, it's been a pleasure to meet you," he said shaking her hand, pulling her into a quick hug.

Marshall opened the doors of the Jeep for his passengers. Once they were buckled in, he rolled down the driveway, turning east onto the road, waving back at the group waving to him at the top of the rise in front of the white farmhouse.

"Finn, I think we should get Daisy. She's had quite a day," Kate said. She immediately received hugs from everyone thrilled with the new woman in Finn's life, and a reminder that they were looking forward to seeing her and her daughter on the Fourth. Kate thanked them for dinner and the invitation.

Finn took her hand, led her into the farmhouse and up the two flights of stairs to Jeli's bedroom. Jeli chattered behind, suggesting Kate bring Daisy over anytime.

Entering Jeli's room, Kate's heart spiked, Finn quickly putting his arm around her. Daisy was curled up on the bed with her arm around Lucas. Both were sleeping soundly exhausted from the day's activities romping through the fields, playing with baby goats, feeding chickens, and playing with each other nonstop.

"I guess we can count your first day on Bradley Farm as being a big success, Kathleen O'Leary. I know a dog who will never be the same … and that goes for me, too." Finn kissed Kate's cheek, then lifted the sleeping child, carrying her downstairs and out to the car. His baby sister bounced heel to toe in anticipation of sharing with her mother that Finn and Kate seemed to be getting along very well. Very well, indeed.

Chapter 22

———

A SWATH OF BRIGHT morning sun cut across the subflooring of the tiny house. A peaceful morning, only the sound of the birds penetrated the green zipboard. Finn leaned against a stud, sipping the last of his coffee. Any moment he expected to see Pops in the doorway ready to begin framing the interior, but right now Finn played over the images of yesterday, letting them swirl through his mind—Daisy playing with the baby goats, Daisy frolicking through the hayfield with Lucas, and Kate smiling at the sound of her daughter's laughter.

It was as if he suddenly had a family. He always thought having a family would be scary, the enormity of lives depending on him. But he wasn't scared. It felt good—he and Kate and Daisy. Even Lucas fit into the picture—a little girl and her puppy.

Finn made a mental note to ask Kate if he could give Lucas to Daisy. They were inseparable yesterday. Finding them curled up together on Jeli's bed, carrying the sleepy child to the car, her arms around his neck, had warmed his heart.

Pops was right. It was possible to fall in love at first sight. The day Kate walked into the tavern to apply for the waitress job he knew she was *the one*.

"Hey, what's going on in there?" Pops called, with joy in his voice.

"Come on in. I was wondering when my foreman was going to show up." Finn watched Pops maneuver up on the small porch.

Another mental note—ask Wolfe to fix a sturdy couple of stairs so Pops could easily navigate in and out of the tiny house.

Grasping the post holding up the overhang, Pops swung up. Georgie and Wolfe were a step behind him, both holding lunchboxes that Wolfe swiped out of the horse barn.

"Jane thought we might need a snack," Wolfe said, setting his pail inside the door.

"Snack? I know you had scrambled eggs with a stack of Gran's special blueberry pancakes before wandering down here," Finn said, chuckling, as he stepped out into the sunlight. "Hey, foreman, what do we do first?"

Pops swung off the porch, again with a grip on the post. "First thing is to unload the appliances and anything else you asked Cameron to load. I cleaned out a staging area in the barn."

"Right-oh," Finn said. "We are all here guys, let's do what the foreman says."

Pops strolled to the back of the barn, pulling the large barn doors open along their tracks. Georgie and Finn started the move with the under-counter refrigerator. "I could almost lift this by myself," Georgie said.

"Probably, but you'd have trouble navigating out the front door. No scratches, bro, after we hauled it without an accident," Finn said.

Setting the fridge on the spot Pops pointed to, Georgie returned for another item as Finn paused to answer his cell.

"Cameron, hi there. We're just unloading the stuff you strapped to the studding. Looks like it all came—"

"Finn, the shop is closed over the Fourth holiday and Carrie and I thought we might take a few extra days off … fly to New Hampshire. We've never been east of the Colorado State line. That is, if it's okay with you?"

"You don't say? It's more than okay," Finn said, grinning, his fingers stroking his scalp, pulling on his piglet.

"Great. We'll reserve a—"

"Oh no, you won't. Don't go reserving a room someplace. You fly into Manchester Airport and Georgie and I'll pick you up.

There's plenty of room in the farmhouse. Mom and Gran will be thrilled to have another bedroom occupied."

"Sounds super. Are you sure it will be fine with Mrs. Bradley?"

"Knock it off, Cam. Mom will be tickled pink to have you. We all will."

"Don't plan anything special. We thought we could lend a hand on your house."

"Can't wait to tell Pops you're coming. He's my foreman, so be ready. He'll talk your ears off—he'll have more questions than a chipmunk has baby pups," Finn said with a chuckle.

"Thanks, Finn. I'll text you with our flight info."

Finn pocketed his cell, turned to gaze at the barn's massive interior. Pops will dwell on questions to ask Cameron, but Finn suddenly felt uneasy. Cameron would question him on his progress for the brewery. Probably get into the nitty-gritty, asking how he was going to repurpose the barn from hay bales and tractors into fermentation tanks.

Sighing, he glanced at his watch. Seven o'clock. Five in the morning in Colorado Springs. Finn smiled. Calling at this hour, I guess the Fosters really are excited about their trip. And I can't wait until they meet Kate. Maybe they're coming as Cameron said—to help with my house.

Finn pulled his hat down against the sun, and followed Georgie back to the green monster for another load of stuff Cameron had tied to the studs.

Chapter 23

Barn to become a brewpub

THE FOSTERS STEPPED OFF the escalator at Manchester Airport into a warm embrace from Finn and Georgie. The new friendship kindled in Colorado Springs less than two weeks ago was real, built on common dreams shared and those yet to be explored. As good friends often do when they're comfortable with each other, there were no stuffy pretenses—all dressed in jeans, polo shirts, and boots, except for Carrie. She wore comfortable sneakers.

Georgie and Finn made quick work retrieving their suitcases. Cam and Carrie seemed to be in a daze, filled with the wonder at being so far from Colorado in a few short hours. Carrie exuberantly chatted about the flight, the terrain they flew over, but most of all she was eager to see a part of the country she'd heard so much about.

The drive from the airport to the farm was filled with question after question from Carrie about the sites whizzing in and out of view—the trees, the quaint towns and the people. Georgie was driving Pops big SUV. Finn asked to borrow the car so everyone would fit comfortably, baggage in the rear.

Cam was content to listen to the give and take between Finn and Georgie as tour guides. Content until Georgie turned up the driveway at Bradley Farm.

Cam first saw the barn labeled Antiques to his right, but when he turned his head to the left, his mouth dropped open.

"Stop! Stop the car," Cam said, the words catching in his throat.

Finn and Georgie thought he was sick from the flight. Georgie stomped on the brake. Cam bolted from the car, came to a halt in the center of the turn into the barn that was to become a brewery, his arms dropping to his side.

Carrie rushed up beside her husband, grasping his hand.

Finn got out of the car letting Georgie drive on up to the house.

"Cam, are you all right?" Finn asked.

"Is that the barn you want to ... where you want to open a brewery?"

"Yep. You don't like it?"

"Like it? It's fantastic. You never said it was this big. And, the land ..." Cam waved his hand as he turned in a circle. "Is this all part of the farm? All yours?"

"Well, it's all part of Bradley Farm—been in the family since 1840. My great, great—"

Cam put both hands in the air to stop Finn mid sentence. He looked at Finn, then sought his wife's eyes. Carrie seemed to be as stunned as her husband.

"Come on, let's walk around back," Finn said, leading the way. "We've only been working on my house for a couple of days, but you'll see Pops has made progress. I hope he didn't bug you too much—all those phone calls he told me he made."

Cam squeezed Carrie's hand. She raised her eyebrows, glancing up at her husband's five-eleven frame. Only a head taller, he kept his eyes on the barn in front of him. He wasn't interested in Finn's tiny house, but he listened politely to what he was saying. Cam was more than intrigued with the barn.

———

THE FOLLOWING DAYS WERE filled with a frenzy of activities between the upcoming holiday, the houseguests, and the fixation on the tiny house and barn. Cameron and Carrie worked alongside Pops and Wolfe, Danny insisting the Fosters call him Pops.

Jeli took off for a meeting in Boston. She called later letting her mom know she was staying at Marshall's condo to watch the fireworks, but would be back before Finn's friends left.

Pops peppered Cam and Carrie about the house details. They in turn peppered Wolfe and Georgie about the farm, particularly the crops, the optimum growing periods, and the makeup of the soil.

Finn and Georgie commented to each other how surprised they were at Carrie's interest in the house and the ideas for the brewery. They attributed it to her support of her husband, and that she was somewhat involved with his home brewing, and, of course, the Fosters had built a tiny house of their own.

Every minute from dawn to noon, before Finn had to go to the tavern, Cam and Carrie were by his side talking beer, beer, and more beer—every aspect of his brewery plans, what Finn knew about the brewery business in New Hampshire, as well as flipping through the various articles and catalogs they brought, adding to what they had given Finn in Colorado Springs. All the time they were talking about beer, they were working on the house.

Pops insisted Georgie take his SUV to ferry his guests around from Lakeville to Portsmouth, and back to the farm, squeezing in some tourist activity. Finn was almost relieved that he had to work overtime at the tavern because of the increased customer traffic, mainly bikers, over the holiday. The big screen TVs on the side wall and over the bar were constantly switched from one baseball double header to another, depending on where the current clusters of bikers were from.

Georgie, eager for a break from his tour-guide duty, was ready for a cold beer and relief from the Foster's never-ending questions. He had called ahead that he was ten minutes away and was stopping with the Fosters for a beer. A burger would also be nice because Gran and Jane were pulling out all stops preparing a picnic feast for their guests tomorrow. Parking in front of the tavern, he was thankful there were only a few motorcycles lined up near the front door. Maybe Finn could take over the inquisition.

Georgie shepherded the Fosters into the Cock & Feathers Tavern. Finn quickly took Kate's hand introducing her to his friends. He was pleasantly surprised when the two women shook hands that ended in a hug.

Georgie had already taken a seat on a barstool and was joined by Cameron. Finn, the happy bartender, served up the first round of beer. Kate and Carrie picked up their glasses and headed to a little table by the front window looking out at a flower box of red geraniums.

"Carrie, you must be exhausted—working on Finn's house and sightseeing today," Kate said.

"A bit. Both Cam and I enjoy poking around, and are enjoying being in New England. How about you, Kate? You don't have the same accent as the Bradley family. Where are you from?"

"Wisconsin. Oops, here come some more customers. Take your beer to the bar, Carrie. I'll join you as soon as I can."

Louie brought out the burger order, joining Finn behind the bar, and was immediately caught up in a question and answer session. Finn deflecting his questions to Louie when it came to how much beer he needed on a monthly basis, the peak times of year, and the favorite blends. These were followed by questions about the competition. Louie couldn't answer him. As far as Louie was concerned, he had no competition. He had all he could handle without trying to drum up new business.

Another wave of bikers entered the tavern and the Fosters said goodbye following Georgie out the door.

Carrie hugged Kate. "See you tomorrow at the farm?"

"Absolutely. Tomorrow," Kate said, with a smile, then hustling to a table with her order pad. The new bikers had reconfigured four tables, pushing them into a big square. Cameron held back, watching the action over his shoulder before joining his wife in the car with Georgie.

Chapter 24

——

THE FOURTH OF JULY holiday was a family affair. Pops, Jane and Gran relished the celebration when their four children were growing up, along with Wolfe and his son Georgie. Today was the first time in a number of years that the house was full of laughter, chatter, and jostling one another, whether playing a game or joking around.

The Fosters were a delight. Cameron was on the quiet side but his mind was constantly churning with ideas. His wife Carrie, on the other hand, was in the thick of the action. Jane whispered to Gran and Carrie, as the three were mixing the potato, melon balls, and pasta salads, that she wished there were more children. But there was at least one child joining in the fun today, Kate's daughter.

Daisy stood ready to put one bowl or platter after another on the kitchen's harvest table, along with ketchup, mustard, and pickles. Lucas followed her from counter to table, waiting patiently by her side until she was called to transfer another dish. The pup was never more than a step away from her.

Wolfe set up the barbeque for Danny, who was in the kitchen mixing up his special sauce for the burgers.

Jane elbowed Gran, nodded for her to look out the window. Finn and Kate were playing badminton with Georgie and Cameron. Finn called for Carrie to relieve him in the game so he could help Pops line up the bratwurst, hot dogs and burgers on the grill. Thankfully the weather had cooperated—nothing but sun, dotted with an occasional cloud puff. It was a perfect day for outdoor activities—sports, grills, and fireworks.

Finn and Kate promised Louie they would take their positions at the tavern by four o'clock. Louie said that was usually the time the bikers rolled in on the holiday to watch a ballgame before heading out to nearby towns for the fireworks. Cameron and Carrie offered to help at the tavern—Cam behind the bar, Carrie helping Kate with the orders and making sure the pitchers of beer were flowing. They knew Louie would cut the bikers off at least thirty minutes before they rolled out, replacing the beer with pots of coffee and pitchers of ice water.

At 3:45, Finn climbed into Georgie's car to drive Kate and the Fosters to the tavern. Georgie would follow in an hour driving Pop's SUV with Wolfe and Jane. There was a Red Sox game they wanted to watch and thought it would be fun to whoop it up with the bikers at the tavern. They planned to stay for the fireworks, switching from Boston to Washington DC, to New York. Gran opted to stay home with Daisy. Daisy loved to play Go Fish, and Gran was happy to sit a spell with the six-year-old.

Finn and Cam had their heads together behind the bar whenever there was a lull. Kate and Carrie kept up a constant chatter, although truncated when taking care of a customer, picking up exactly where they left off. When the first group of bikers were taken care of, beer, burgers, and fries, the pair relaxed at a corner table to the side of the bar. Kicking off their shoes, wiggling their toes while they had a chance. Earlier, at the farm, they laughed seeing that they both chose to wear a black sundress—Carrie a sheath dress, Kate a halter dress, both with black flats for comfort.

"Finn is good for Cam," Carrie said looking over at her husband in an animated conversation behind the bar. "I haven't seen him so excited … ever."

"What do you do, Carrie, while Cam builds houses?" Kate asked.

"I guess you'd call me a people person in a high-tech firm. I'm a manager in the Human Resource Department."

"Sounds challenging. Do you have children?"

"No. We're waiting to start a family … saving money."

"Oh, oh. Up and at 'em, girlfriend. I hear the roar of more bikers," Kate said.

Cameron looked over at the girls putting on their shoes. "Finn, I was wondering … if it isn't an imposition … please say if it is … anyway, Carrie and I thought we'd stay a few more days. I think, with all of your family's help, that we can almost finish your house, except for the painting, staining. We could have your hookups in place for the electrical and water. Your Pops said the septic tank company was coming in a couple of weeks so we have to wait on that, but I can do the other in my sleep. And, I brought some notes, my research for your brewery, that I'd like to share with you … do a back-of-the-envelope layout for the barn."

"Are you kidding? I'd love it."

"I think you're sitting on a big opportunity—the farm, the barn, the land. You have a big leg up on fixed expenses. You can even grow your own barley and hops. I mentioned it to Georgie, and he said he'd start researching the crops on his computer. I found that New Hampshire passed some new regulations to help the craft brewer entrepreneur movement sweeping across the country. I also found a template for a business plan for a startup brewery in New Hampshire."

"Tomorrow morning, first thing, I'd like to see what you found," Finn said, looking at the man who just strolled into the tavern.

It was Scarface. He strode passed the bar into the kitchen area. Finn watched him pick up Louie, pushing him against the wall. He barely heard him, over the chatter of the bikers, threatening Louie, saying again he wanted the bitcoins. Louie's eyes wide in terror, said they were his. Finn thought he heard Scarface say something like, "… not any more. I'll be back."

Dropping Louie to the floor, he strolled out of the kitchen and left the tavern.

Finn looked through the order window at Louie. He seemed frozen in place. "What's going on?"

"Nothing. Go back to work."

Louie tried to brush the encounter with Scarface off, but Finn wasn't exactly buying it, making a note to himself to have a chat with Louie. No one should push him around that way.

The place was packed by eight o'clock. The ballgame ended and Finn saw an opportunity for an impromptu jam session, singing and dancing. He hustled to the back room, changing into a ruffled shirt, rhinestone trousers cinched with his rhinestone belt. Strutting out to the bar with his guitar, he jumped up on a table and began strumming. Two bikers raced outside, returning with their guitars, joining Finn with foot-tapping country music. Music rose to the rafters, bikers singing and dancing, embracing the holiday spirit.

Tables were pushed back, men pulled partners to the dance floor, then everyone joining in a conga line, Pops included. One biker grabbed Jane's hand drawing her into the line. Georgie, who rarely danced, led the procession in and out of the tables, tugging Louie in the line still wearing his apron, weaving around behind the bar and back out to the floor again, finally collapsing on their chairs.

Word spread that it was time to be on their way or they'd miss the fireworks. Suddenly it was quiet in the tavern. The only noise came from the two televisions beginning the broadcast of the holiday celebrations across the country.

Fifteen minutes into the Boston display, Georgie offered to drive the exhausted tiny house foreman and his wife home. The Fosters said that sounded like a good idea, saying goodnight to Louie, then Kate and Finn.

Louie, still shaken from Scarface's threat, asked Finn to lock up, and he'd appreciate it if he and Kate stayed to tidy up the tavern, mainly put the tables and chairs back in place.

———

IT HAD BEEN A wonderful day because Kate was part of it, always in his line of sight. Finally they were alone in the tavern. Most of the table candles were extinguished, the remaining lined up on the bar, creating a cozy, romantic atmosphere. Finn punched several buttons on the jukebox, picking out tunes for slow dancing. He wanted to hold Kate, sway with her in his arms. Seeing she had kicked off her shoes again, he liked the idea and pulled his boots off behind the bar.

Kate put the last spatula away in the drawer beside Louie's grill and stepped around to the bar to join Finn. He picked up her hand, gently pulling her to him, bending his head, his cheek against hers.

"Have fun today?" he whispered.

Snuggling closer in his arms, she ran her fingers over his shoulders. "Oh, yes. I've never had a better Fourth."

He clasped her arm sliding down to her hand, twirling her out and back into a long embrace. Tucking her head under his chin, he swayed to the music.

"Katie, I'm falling in love with you. Can you see yourself here … on the farm?"

Kate didn't answer, but her body language spoke volumes, her hands circling his neck, fingering his piglet. Her eyes were warm but he thought there was a hint of sadness.

Standing on tiptoe, she kissed him.

He stopped swaying, holding her in his arms, his breathing labored.

She hadn't answered his question.

"Can you think about it? I'm sorry I blurted out my feelings … I couldn't hold back any longer. Can you … see yourself here … with me?"

"I—"

"Just think about it, will you?"

Kate nodded.

Again, he saw pain in her eyes. *She wants to say yes, but something is holding her back.*

Chapter 25

———

FINN DID NOT REVEAL his declaration of love for Kate to anyone, but it was obvious to the family that something happened last night. Maybe not lovers in the strict sense of the word, but lovers none the less,—a touch, a smile, a peck on the cheek. He picked up Kate and Daisy every morning, bringing them to the construction site. Kate and Carrie worked side by side, close like they'd known each other for a long time.

Work on Finn's house proceeded with renewed vigor after the celebration of the Fourth. With the Foster's decision to stay on for a week, Pops sketched out a daily plan, keeping the crew working at breakneck speed. It was a good thing he had the necessary tools and equipment pre-positioned in the barn so not a moment was lost. The electric saw hummed cutting the boards for the siding—inside and out. Hammers pounded nails, and electric screwdrivers made quick work installing windows, cabinets, and the loft.

Gran and Jane knew something was up, but had no idea of the magnitude of the crew's exertion trying to keep to Pop's work schedule. The pair trudged down the driveway every couple of hours, a carafe of coffee swinging from Jane's hand, a tote with foam cups, creamers, sugar and napkins over Gran's shoulder. The only information they gleaned from Danny was that Cameron and Carrie thought with all hands on deck they had a shot at finishing, or at least coming close to finishing construction before they flew back to Colorado.

One night Cameron was so tired that he went to bed as the sun set. He needed to be up at dawn because he just knew, felt it in his bone-weary body, that the little house would be ready to move in before they left.

Georgie was like a boomerang shot from the construction site to the tree house on the back edge of the property where he and his dad lived, returning with a printout to show Finn and Cam. When Gran questioned Wolfe about what his son was doing, all he knew was something he overheard about new crops. Barley? Hops?

As for Finn and Cameron, they would disappear into the barn for fifteen or thirty minutes with a cup of coffee, heads together, bent over some sort of catalogs. Shiny steel tanks were all Wolfe saw, glancing over his shoulder one afternoon.

The third day seemed to slow up a bit. The job of foreman was transferred to Cameron for the temporary hookup of electricity and water from the barn, and the attachment of a storage tank ready to be connected to the septic tank scheduled for installation in another week.

Cameron and Georgie surprised Finn that night when he came home from his shift at the tavern to see lights shining inside his house. At Cameron's urging to step inside to test the water hookup, Finn turned on the kitchen faucet, and then the bathroom's shower, grinning at the sight of water streaming from the fixtures. Georgie demonstrated boiling water on the stove, and opened the under-counter refrigerator revealing a six-pack of beer. The little freezer compartment held doughnuts for tomorrow's first coffee break.

Finn, at a loss for words, just shook his head. He couldn't believe the progress.

Kate and Carrie disappeared on day four. Borrowing Danny's SUV, they went shopping. They returned to the farm with a car full of bags—a small set of pans, colorful dishes, and bedding from Walmart. Two large cartons were strapped to the roof of the car.

Foam mattresses—queen for the loft, and a twin for the downstairs bedroom. They explained to Finn that he could store the smaller mattress, ready to haul out for an occasional guest. Otherwise the space could be an office or whatever. Because the girls didn't know his taste in furnishings, they purchased the basics in bright colors. Heck, why not? He could always return or exchange the items. Carrie had seen models at the manufacturer so she had a good idea of what worked.

One day morphed into the next and with only one more day before the Foster's were leaving, Jeli pitched in brushing the final coat of preservative on the exterior cedar siding covering the green zipboard. Jane watched the money dwindle from Finn's line of credit at the bank. She feared he wasn't going to have enough, but with Cam's experience it looked like there was a chance they would finish before the money ran out. Finn had planned how he was going to cover the payments from his job at the tavern. No one dared say anything when, at the last minute, he had to dip into his meager savings for the brewery. They didn't want to put a wet blanket on his excitement.

Finn didn't know if he was coming or going during the week, but he loved having Kate work along with the crew, and also knowing they were going to be together at the tavern. On several days, Daisy stayed at the farmhouse playing with Lucas. When Finn and Kate bid goodbye to the construction crew, they piled into his truck, making one stop on the way to the tavern. They dropped off an exhausted Daisy for an afternoon nap under the care of Mrs. Peters.

Driving Kate home after their shift was the best part of Finn's day. The part when he and Kate spent time together, alone. He'd park the truck in her driveway, holding her hand while they chatted. Walking her to the door, he'd wrap her in his arms with a long embrace. Even though the last kiss of the night was warm, there was a veil of sadness in her eyes as she said goodnight, entering the house, shutting the door.

Chapter 26

———

IT SEEMED SO SUDDEN. At the farm eating tuna fish sandwiches for lunch, adrenalin pumping to complete the finishing touches on the tiny house, and now hustling down the jetway to board the 4:35 p.m. return flight to Colorado Springs.

Carrie scooted into the window seat as Cameron, stuffing their carryon bags into the overhead bin, flopped down beside her. Seatbelts buckled, they both sighed, heads pressed against the seatback. The jet taxied down the runway and then rose into the sky, heading for Chicago. Once they landed in Chicago, they had a little over an hour to catch the connecting flight, expecting to land at COS Airport at 8:59 p.m.

Cameron reached for his wife's hand, holding on tightly. He needed an anchor, reassurance that she was by his side, knowing the decision he was struggling with, a decision that would change the course of their lives.

The visit to Bradley Farm had been a heady experience—the rural beauty of New Hampshire, the warm hospitality of the Bradley clan—a tight, loving family. Cameron had never experienced such love of family. Because of this and the opportunity he saw, he was struggling with a decision of whether or not to broach the subject of a possible partnership with Finn. If Finn's mind was set on going it alone, establishing a brewery on the farm, then there was no decision to be made. The Fosters would stay in Colorado Springs. The dream of starting their own brewery would probably never be more than that—a dream.

The cabin attendants made their way down the aisle dispensing beverages and peanuts. Carrie sipped her coffee, her eyes peeled out the window at the acres of farmland below, one to the other. Then a city with traffic congestion, nothing like the peace she experienced in New Hampshire. She didn't dare look at Cam for fear she would interrupt his thought process. He was an intense man, one who anguished over decisions large and small. "Decisions have consequences," he said many times. "One must be as sure as can be before making a decision."

They loved each other, cared deeply for each other. In spite of coming from different backgrounds, they had made their marriage work. Cameron grew up in Colorado Springs, a son of a neighborhood grocer. Both his mother and father worked at the store, bickering daily. He and his younger sister often worked in the store, both vowing to move east or west to start a different life as soon as they could manage.

Cameron had decided early on that he would never work with his wife, when he had a wife. He didn't like the constant quarrels between his parents. They couldn't afford to send him to college which was just fine with Cameron. He had ideas of his own and didn't want to spend hours, years, in a field of study he saw as meaningless. He took every shop class offered in high school and was hired by a developer after graduation as part of the man's building team. The job served as an apprenticeship for what was to come—a position with a new enterprise.

A new builder started a business designing, manufacturing, and selling a new type of house, a tiny house. The tiny house was marketed as an RV on a trailer. It was quaint, cost effective, and filled with new ideas, taking advantage of every available space inside and outside. They became very popular for two segments of the population—young adults who couldn't afford large mortgages but who could pay cash for a tiny house eliminating monthly payments. The second segment consisted of retirees who sold their large empty nest, and with the equity paid cash for their new home. The new buyer either hit the road, traveling as they had dreamed before retirement, or set the house on a plot of land near a lake, a river, on the top of a mountain—whatever suited them.

Cameron knew the advantages of being frugal. He was a saver. A tiny house suited him to a Tee.

Turbulence shook the plane causing it to drop several feet. Cam squeezed Carrie's hand, reassuring her that everything was alright. Her breathing returned to normal as the apprehension passed.

Turning back to the window, Carrie's thoughts went to her parents. How would they take her moving to New England? Maybe not so bad. For the past ten years her mom and dad had formed a partnership selling real estate. They worked seamlessly together, and pretty much left their three children, two boys and a girl, Carrie being the middle child, to fend for themselves. Plus, unlike Cameron's parents, they would be able to afford a flight, now and again, to visit the east coast ... if they wanted to.

Carrie's thoughts turned to her job, wondered about pulling up stakes with her husband, leaving a career she had worked hard to achieve. She left the family home in Denver to attend the University in Colorado Springs, graduating with a degree in business. She remained in the Springs, and now held a responsible job as Manager of Human Resources in a high-tech firm.

Glancing at her husband, his head rested on her shoulder, his eyes closed. He finally let go of the decision he was puzzling through, or maybe he had solved his dilemma. Either way, she knew they would discuss the pros and cons on the next and last leg of their flight.

She smiled dismissing the urge to kiss his cheek, tell him they would work it through together, but she didn't dare take the chance of waking him. He needed his rest after the furious pace of trying to finish Finn's tiny house before they left. He came close. Only a couple of items were left, like a doorknob, a light fixture over the bathroom sink.

Watching her husband breathe easily, her mind retraced how they met. Carrie fell head over heels for Cameron and he for her at an event her company held in a brewpub on the outskirts of town. They confessed to each other a year later that they both knew that night that they had found their soul mate. She made more money than he, but they agreed on the percentage to save from their combined salaries. Unbeknownst to Cameron, Carrie put three times as much into another savings account, an account adding up to fund his dream, bring his dream into reality.

One thing was for sure, they didn't have to worry about where they would live. They had downsized two years ago to a tiny house. Carrie smiled thinking of the size of Bradley Farm. If Cameron did go into partnership with Finn, they could probably put their tiny house on the farm. If not, then the decision was easy—they would remain in Colorado.

In her heart, Carrie hoped they would move. She wanted a baby. Cameron did as well but felt unsettled and wanted to wait. When his dream materialized, then it would be time to start a family.

Carrie was way ahead of him in planning the future. They would trailer their tiny house to Bradley Farm, where he and Finn would put the plans together and start the renovation on the barn for the brewpub. She would return to Colorado Springs for six months and then join her husband. Maybe the senior Fosters would let her bunk on their couch, saving even more money to invest in the brewery.

Sighing, Carrie let go of the thoughts that had played out in her mind. If all failed, Colorado Springs was a beautiful place to live. And staying meant they could start a family, in her mind anyway.

The plane began the descent into Chicago's O'Hare International Airport. Grinning, Cam leaned across the armrest and kissed his wife's cheek.

Yes indeed, the next leg of the flight was going to be interesting. Her husband had made a decision and appeared eager to get her approval.

———

THEY HAD BEEN HOME a week, and Carrie kept nudging Cam to call Finn. All her husband had done since returning to Colorado was pace—before going to his job at the tiny house builder, and after work when he returned home.

In his research on the internet, he found a farmer in Georgia who was working on methods to store grain and hops. Cameron was eager to share with Finn the possibility of growing their own crops.

Cam was constantly sketching layouts for the barn, including placement of the bar, tables and booths with a wall of glass allowing the patrons to see the brewing process. He sketched a flow chart—grinding the grain, the brewing and fermentation tanks, with all the steps between, and then the packaging and distribution of the bottles. They definitely needed to configure a tasting room ... and a tap room.

He was constantly rearranging the sketches for the greatest impact, all part of the proposal he was going to pitch to Finn. The plan had to be well thought-out, especially including how they might proceed as partners. One thing he didn't want to do was scare Finn.

Working through the sequence of the proposal with Carrie, they put together a chart for the presentation. But Cameron would not proceed with the proposal unless Finn seemed to buy in to the idea—going into business together as partners.

Cameron and Carrie had already decided that, if the partnership was a go, they would invest their savings. The savings they had hoped one day to fund their own brewery, they would invest with Finn on Bradley Farm.

Or, if it wasn't a go, they would remain in Colorado Springs!

Chapter 27

———

NO SMILING KATE THIS AFTERNOON. She barely said hello to him. Finn kept glancing her way as she took the orders from the first group of seven bikers and then a party of four eager for a respite from the road. Nor did she look at him when rattling off the beer requests before turning to Louie at the order window—eleven burgers with fries.

Finn touched her arm and was startled at the gloom written on her face. Her eyes had lost their sparkle and her mouth was definitely turned down at the corners.

"Hey, babe, what's the matter?" Finn said, his eyes seeking hers.

"Nothing. Everything." She picked up a tray of glasses for the bikers and the table of four, forcing her lips to turn up in a rigid smile.

But the smile flipped to a frown when she returned for the pitchers of beer, then back and forth to the order window for the burgers and fries. The guests were now content—drinking, eating, between bouts of laughter. Kate returned to the side of the doorway next to the bar, leaned back, absently checking a fingernail.

Finn sauntered from the back of the bar, leaned his head against the wall next to Kate. "Are you going to tell me what's wrong or do we play twenty questions?"

"I've been evicted. Daisy and I. We have to be out by the weekend."

"When did this happen?"

"Mrs. Peters told me a month ago."

"A month?" Finn said, stroking her cheek. "Why didn't you say something?"

"I was going to but the Fourth was coming up. I thought she'd change her mind. But no way was that going to happen. She said her sister and husband were coming to visit for the summer ... maybe longer ... and then the Fosters came ... and you were flat out ... I didn't want to bother you. I've looked for something close to the tavern ... nothing." A tear escaped her eye, dropping to her blouse.

Finn grasped her elbow, marching her to the backroom, holding her in his arms. "It's going to be okay. I'll help ... somehow." He gently swiped his thumb under her eye as another tear dropped to her cheek.

"No, no. It's probably time for Daisy and I to move on—"

"Oh no, you don't. You're not leaving here. You're not leaving me. Hold on. Let me think," he said, tucking her head under his chin.

Taking her hand, Finn sat her down on a stack of grain bags, snatched his man-size handkerchief from his back pocket. "I'll be right back. Don't you move." He handed her the red square of cloth and walked out of the room.

"Louie, we have to do something."

"And, what do we have to do?"

"Did Kate tell you she was leaving?"

"What? She can't do that. The customers love her. You see those bikers? They're here every Thursday just because of her, I swear. Why would she leave?"

"She doesn't have a place to live ... something about the place she's at now is taken because someone's sister ... long story. I have an idea. My tiny house is finished. How about I park it, temporarily, out back in that cluster of pine trees? The water and electricity hookups are close enough. Pops and Georgie can make it work. I bet you anything they can. What do you say?"

"I have no problem with that ... temporarily."

"You're a good man, Louie," Finn said, giving Louie's shoulder a punch. "I'll see if it's okay with Kate ... call Pops ... day after tomorrow ... she'll be all set," Finn muttered, hustling back to Kate.

Kneeling in front of her, he flashed a big smile. "It's all set ... that is, if you want to."

Kate blew her nose. "What's all set?" She folded the large piece of cloth and put it in her pocket. "Thanks, I'll wash it."

"You know, my house that—"

"Of course, I know your house ... very well. I do believe that Carrie and I shopped for all the stuff in that house. Did you forget—"

"Right," he said grinning. *She's going to love this.* "And ... you know that it's finished, well, we have to put everything you and Carrie bought inside, and Georgie still has to install a light in the bathroom. That won't take long, and then—"

"Finn Bradley, you're not making any sense. What does your house, with or without the light, the bedding, dishes, etcetera, etcetera, have to do with—"

"It has to do with you and Daisy. Louie said Pops and Georgie can move it into that spot of pine trees out back. Come on I'll show you." Finn pulled her to her feet, hugged her quick, kissed her quick, then dragged her along, striding outside, down to the back edge of the tavern's parking lot and stopped short. "There. Right there."

"You're not thinking ..."

"Yup. We'll hook her up right there ... in two days ... three at the most. Louie said you can stay as long as you want ... temporarily."

Kate's brows shot up, her big blue eyes searching his face. "Are you kidding?"

"Hey, would I kid you?"

"As a matter of fact, all the time." Kate threw her arms around him. "I love it. I love it."

Finn would have been happier if she had said she loved him. But what the heck, if she loved his house, could he be far behind?

Kate suddenly stepped back, raised her palms in the air at him. "On one condition."

"And that is?"

"When you're ready to move in because the brewery is ready—"

"You worry too much. On the other hand it would make a great, high-stakes rock-paper-scissors game. Definitely two out of three."

"Make that three out of five." Kate giggled, as Finn picked her up, twirled her around, followed with a hot kiss that sent his hat flying.

Chapter 28

*Tiny House
ready to move in*

BIG RED SLOWLY BACKED the tiny house into its temporary home surrounded by a stand of trees behind the tavern's parking lot. Finn gripped the wheel, watching the hands waving in the mirrors, rearview and side—a foot left, a smidge to the right.

Wolfe and Georgie threw up their palms. "That's it. Stop. Stop," they shouted.

"Perfect," Georgie yelled.

Louie stood next to Kate, hands on his head, fingers laced. "The green tank has turned into a dollhouse. Who would've thought? So different finished. Same size, of course," he said grinning.

"Just wait until Finn shows you around inside," Kate said sheltering her eyes from the late morning sun.

Pops turned into the parking lot tooting his horn as he stopped behind Georgie's car. Boxes were stacked in his SUV and Georgie's green Chevy.

"Where do you want all this, Kate?" Pops asked, climbing out of his vehicle.

"Louie said we can put the boxes in the backroom of the tavern, easy access for me to set up the house," Kate said, her eyes scanning the boxes she could see through the open car window.

"Right-oh," Pops said.

Everyone turned at the line of bikers roaring in front of the tavern. Parking their bikes, jostling each other, laughing as they entered the front door.

"Back to business, Finn," Louie said, hustling in the back door, his short, wide body bouncing with each step.

"We'll move the boxes, Kate. You and Finn go *take care of business,*" Georgie said chuckling. "I filled up the water tank last night, forty gallons, so the utilities work just like an RV, except for the electricity. Finn, you and I can deal with your truck tomorrow. No need to unhitch her now. Looks like you're going to be busy behind the bar."

"Thanks, Georgie. Sounds good. And, thank you, Wolfe, for all your help."

Kate hustled to Finn's side. "Georgie, I told Daisy she could spend the first night with me, so—"

"Don't you worry, Kate. Finn already put the regular mattress in the little bedroom, and the queen with the bedding in the loft before he left the farm. I'll drive Daisy here. What time do you think?"

"9:30 would be great. Is that too late for you?"

"Nope. 9:30 it is. See you later," Georgie said.

Kate waved goodbye as Finn drew her up on her tiptoes for a quick kiss. Settling her back down, he grasped her hand turning to his truck, the house behind. All he could see was the roofline with the two skylights above the loft.

"What do you think, Katie? Cozy?"

"I love it. I can't believe you came up with the idea … your new house … nobody's ever been so kind …

"Hey, no tears."

One more kiss and they darted in the door *to get back to business.*

Chapter 29

———

THE TAVERN WAS PACKED. Louie brought out every available chair including two kitchen chairs from his upstairs apartment. At times, someone vacated a barstool only to be immediately occupied by a quick-witted biker standing against the wall. Patrons were content to watch one baseball game after the other—New York, Seattle, Miami, Detroit. The mid-July temperature reached the nineties by two o'clock—too hot even for the most avid biker. Kate wanted to dive into the boxes of dishes and pans that she and Carrie had picked out, but there was no down time between taking orders and serving pitchers of beer, plates of burgers and fries, along with the occasional order of Fenway Franks when the Red Sox were playing.

Finn glanced to his left as Scarface hitched up on a barstool vacated by a biker hustling to the men's room, thinking his spot would be saved. His friend shrugged when the man with a scar down his face commandeered the stool.

"Hey, bartender, tell Shorty that Scarface is here to see him."

"And just who might Shorty be?" Finn asked, pushing his hat up high on his forehead. *Blast. It was a good day until this creep came in.*

"Very funny, but I'm not laughing. Now go tell your boss I'm here. We have a little business to settle and I'm tired of waiting. Tell him I'm tired of his games."

"He sees you."

Louie was peeking above the sill of the order window, his eyes wide then slipping out of sight.

Scarface grinned. "I know he does. I'll just go have a chat with him. Help him flip those burgers."

"I don't think—"

Finn didn't have a chance to finish what he was saying. Scarface was nose to nose with Louie, pushing the little fat man against the doorframe of the cooking center. Suddenly Scarface picked Louie up under his armpits, smashing him against the edge of the doorway between the shoulder blades.

Louie, eyes buggy, shook his head at whatever Scarface was saying. His feet dangling, fear gripping his pudgy body.

Scarface dropped him, causing Louie to fall to his knees. Scarface muttered as Louie tried to stand, backing away on his butt toward the backroom. Scarface, his face contorted, as if smelling shit, turned on his heel, striding out of the tavern.

Kate's eyes followed Scarface, as she let out a sigh of relief.

Finn hurried around the corner to help Louie to his feet. "Here, give me your hand."

Louie grasped Finn's hand, letting Finn pull him up. "I'm OK. Go back to the bar. Go on. Don't fuss. Don't say anything to Kate—"

"She saw him, Louie. That guy's no good. He assaulted you, for god's sake. I'm calling the police."

"No, no. It's not your problem, Finn. I said go back to the bar."

Shaking his head, Finn reluctantly did what he was told.

The Red Sox catcher hit a home run with the bases loaded in the bottom of the ninth. Happy fans rocked the tavern. Everyone jumped to their feet, yelling, pumping fists, slapping each other's hands, calling for more pitchers of beer, as Louie disappeared into the backroom.

Televisions were changed to another channel, to another game. The crowd was having a gay old time but began switching from beer to sodas, water, or coffee, anything without alcohol, sobering up to roll.

Louie emerged, peeked around the corner, motioning to Finn to follow him to the storage area.

"Are you all right, Louie? I still think—"

"I told you, I'm okay. Here, take this," Louie said, shoving a large briefcase into Finn's chest. "Hide it. Keep it safe. If anything happens to me, it's yours." Louie removed a gold key from his key ring, pushing it into Finn's hand.

Chapter 30

———

THE SUDDEN SILENCE IN the tavern was palpable. Shadows crept around chairs, table legs, shifting across the walls and ceiling, as Kate methodically extinguished the candles. At ten o'clock the bikers had cleared out in mass, exhausted from cheering their teams on. It was time to leave the tavern's stale air, time to breathe in the fresh fragrance of the night, feel it against their faces as they jumped on the gas, hitting the road.

With only a few candles on the bar, Kate perched on a stool, kicking off her white sneakers dabbed with spots of ketchup. Bending over, she rubbed the toes on her right foot. Finn came around the bar, knelt in front of her taking over massaging her toes. Without glancing up, he whispered, "Scarface really freaked Louie out."

"I saw, but I don't know why," she whispered in return.

"Me either. There, does that feel better?" Finn asked, slipping her sneakers back on her slender feet.

"Umm, ever so much better. Thanks. Why are you calling that man Scarface ... a nickname I suppose with—"

"Louie says that's what people call him. Anyway, after Scarface left, Louie asked me to take care of a briefcase for him."

"What's in it?"

"He didn't say." Finn hitched up on the barstool next to Kate, leaned on his elbow facing her, tenderly tracing her cheek with his finger. Leaning closer, he touched his lips to hers. She was so pretty in the flickering candlelight. He wanted to draw her close—

"What did you do with it … the briefcase?"

He paused to catch his breath before answering. "I stashed it under the mattress in the loft … for now."

"Under the mattress?" she said in a normal voice. "Really?"

"Shh. Well, well to one side. It won't bother you and Daisy."

"Can I move it … if it gives me a headache?" she said, rubbing her forehead, feigning pain.

"I'll think about it," he said grinning. "I hear Georgie and Daisy. It's time to tuck you girls into bed in your new home."

"Anybody here?" Georgie called out softly entering the bar from the backroom. He was carrying a sleeping angel in his arms.

"Right here, Georgie," Finn whispered, glancing over at his friend.

"How about I tuck Daisy in the loft? I'll wait for you on the porch," Georgie said.

"That would be great. Kate and I were just talking. It was a crazy busy day, and I don't know, the candles—"

"Not another word," Georgie said, grinning as he left.

Kate blew out the candles as Finn checked that the front door was locked. Taking her hand, Finn locked up as they left the tavern through the back door. Georgie was waiting as promised on the porch, as they walked up to him.

"Finn?" Kate put her hand on his chest, her eyes telling him she had something serious on her mind.

"Yesss?"

"Can I ask you a favor?"

"Ask away, babe."

"Could you stay with Daisy and me tonight? I'm a little unnerved at being alone in the woods, and after Scarface … Daisy and I will give you the loft. We can fit in the little bedroom."

"Well, maybe all three of us could sleep in the loft?"

"Nice try, but I don't think so," Kate said with a half smile.

"Now that you've settled the sleeping arrangements, I guess I'm odd man out. However, you owe me big time. It wasn't easy going up the tiny stairs with a six-year-old holding a mother kangaroo with a baby in its pouch. See you guys tomorrow … sometime. Nighty night," Georgie said grinning.

"Come on, Katie. Give me your hand. Your gladiator is ready to protect," Finn said, slapping Georgie on the back. "Thanks, bro. See you tomorrow."

Entering the tiny house, Kate scampered up the stairs built against the wall, each step built on a pull-out drawer.

"Are you going to sleep in your clothes?" Finn asked.

"No, silly. I have pajamas under my pillow. A damsel in her turret must be prepared for all eventualities."

Finn stepped to the kitchen sink. "Do you want a glass of water? There's a cup holder on the bedside table for—"

"You and Cameron thought of everything. Can you hand it up to me?" Kate scrunched around, both arms hanging over the edge of the loft. Did you know that your mom and Gran offered to let Daisy stay on the farm during the week?"

"No, I didn't know, but I'm not surprised. Lucas will be thrilled." Finn handed her the water glass. Cocking his head to the side, he turned to go into the little bedroom. "It's a good thing Louie has floodlights in the parking lot so we can see. Georgie and I'll get the electricity hooked up in the morning."

"Thanks for the water. Night."

"You're welcome. Night, back at you."

Chapter 31

———

SO COZY.

So peaceful.

Kate could hear the male crickets chirping, scraping their wings hoping to attract a female. Maybe this is where she was meant to be. Her life scripted, starting a new page in New Hampshire. She and Daisy. Turning on her side, Kate looked out the little dormer window at the moon, its beams of silver light …

Daisy rolled against her, touching her arm. "Aunt Kate, are you awake?"

"I sure am, sweet girl. I heard you were Gran's little helper today."

"I guess so. She made a salad and I cut up the carrots and tomatoes and green peppers. It was very colorful and I didn't cut my finger."

"Do you like it here, Daisy … on the farm?"

"Oh, yes. Everyone is so nice, especially Gran. She lets me help her in the kitchen … so does Jane." Daisy sat up, arms hugging her legs.

"How about Finn? Do you like him?" Kate asked, leaning on her elbow.

"I like him the best. He's very funny and he treats me like a big person. He said I'm in charge of Lucas when I'm on the farm. I wish Lucas could stay with us, here in this house. Do you like Finn, Aunt Kate?"

"Yes, I do."

"A whole bunch?"

"Yes, a whole bunch. Guess what you can help me with in the morning?"

"What ... will it be fun?"

"I think so. You and I, missy, will unpack the boxes with all the pretty things Carrie and I bought for Finn. We're going to decorate this little house."

"That will be way fun."

"Now, you lie down and try to go to sleep. Want to snuggle with me?"

"Uh huh."

Kate drew Daisy against her, folding her into her arms. The little girl had been through so much, she wanted to hold her tight, love her. Kate kissed the top of her head, her soft blonde hair. *I'll take care of you, Daisy. I'll protect you. I promise.*

Chapter 32

———

WHAT WAS THAT?

Kate raised her head.

Scooched up on her elbows.

Cocked her head ... listening.

A car door?

Rolling over she looked out the window. She couldn't see a car in the parking lot.

There was no headroom to stand, so she scooted to the edge of the loft. Dragging her pillow, plumping it under her elbows, she looked down. *Maybe Finn forgot something in the truck.*

Kate felt the house jerk.

Jerked again.

Are we moving? What's Finn doing?

Suddenly Finn's shadow appeared, standing in the great room. He was gripping the edge of the staircase. His T-shirt and boxer shorts were stark white for a second in the moonlight, then only a shadow.

The house picked up speed.

Finn looked up. He saw Kate for a split second in the moonlight, looking down at him.

"Kate ... we're moving."

"How ... what's happening?"

"I don't know."

"Who's driving? If Georgie is playing a joke, it's not funny." Her tone was huffy.

"That bump ... at the end of the driveway ... we're turning left ..."

"Finn, we're going really fast."

"Aunt Kate, why are we moving? Are we leaving again?" Daisy whispered, crawling up beside her aunt.

"Kate, someone is stealing my house," Finn said.

Kate quickly crawled back with Daisy, wrapping them together in the sheet. Twisting, she looked out the window only inches away. Silhouettes of trees were whizzing by.

"Kate, can you hear me?"

"Yes, I hear you."

"Whoever is stealing the house probably doesn't know we're in here. He'll ... if it's a he ... must be a he. He might look inside when he stops. Get dressed and be sure to put your shoes on. Daisy too. You have to be very quiet. I have the flashlight. I'll stand by the door. If he comes inside, I'll knock him over the head."

"Finn, this is NOT funny. If you're playing a joke—"

"I'm NOT playing a joke. After you get dressed, scrunch down with Daisy so he won't see you, so he won't know you're in the loft."

Chapter 33

———

THE MOON WAS GONE, covered by thickening clouds as the little house sped along the road.

"Kate? Daisy? Are you kiddos undercover?" Finn whispered.

"Where did you go?" Kate whispered into the black air.

"I couldn't find the flashlight. When I took off my jeans I laid it on the bed. Without it … don't worry, I found it."

"What if you miss … you know, hitting the person on the head?"

"Don't you worry, babe, I was QB for my high school team. When I threw a pass I always hit the mark."

"We're turning again," Kate whispered.

"Hang on, it's really bumpy. Do you know what time it is?"

"Really, Finn. The time? My cell is my purse. I have to find my purse … I think …"

"Never mind. I'd say we're on a dirt road. Maybe we're on Bradley Farm, and—"

"Finn, if we get out of this alive, I have something to tell you."

"Uh. What's it about?"

"Daisy and I …"

"Whoa! Hang on. We stopped … I can still hear Big Red … we're moving again … really slow … the engine's stopped. Remember, not a word."

"Right," Kate said, pulling the sheet up over her nose, her eyes darting around in the inky black loft.

"Hear that?" Finn whispered.

"What is it?"

"A barn door sliding on the rails."

Then, no sound.

No crickets.

No moon.

Nothing but black air cloaked the tiny house.

"Kate?" Finn whispered.

"Yes."

"I think whoever moved the barn door left." Finn stepped into the great room waving the flashlight. "Come on down. We have to get out of here. If he comes back, we'd be trapped."

"Right. Come on, Daisy. Finn, stop waving the flashlight, you're making me dizzy. Shine it on the stairs or we'll fall for sure."

"Oh. Yea, right."

First Daisy, then Kate stepped down from the loft into Finn's arms.

"You kiddos okay?"

"You asked us that before."

"Well?"

"Yes, we're okay. Now what?"

"Out the door."

"Finn, I can't see."

"Sorry. Let me go first. Oh, oh. No stepstool off the porch. I'll jump."

"Be careful," Kate said, her hand on Finn's back as he disappeared into a black hole.

"Finn, where are you?"

"Here." He chuckled, turning the flashlight up on his face, his lips in a ghoulish grin.

"Stop trying to scare us, Finn. We're not in the mood are we, Daisy."

"You look creepy, Finn," Daisy said, clutching Kate's hand.

"Sorry. Here's the flashlight, now hand Daisy down to me. Good, that's my-girl," he said setting Daisy on her feet. "Your turn,

Katie. Hand me the flashlight and bend down. Put your hands on my shoulders—"

Kate kicked off the front porch knocking Finn on his butt.

"Whoa. Knocked me flat," Finn said, laughing as he grasped Kate's hand helping him to his feet.

Picking up the flashlight, he waved it around their prison. "Looks like a big old barn. Bigger than the biggest barn on the farm. Come on, up that ladder over there to the first hayloft just in case that guy comes back. I'll climb up first, give you a hand up. I'll call Georgie ... tell him where we are."

"And where do you suppose that is?" Kate asked helping Daisy to the first rung of the ladder. She grabbed Finn's hand, climbed up the ladder, and then Finn gave Kate a hand up.

He twirled a beam of light around the barn. "Let's hide over there, behind those bales. If he comes back with a flashlight, or if there's a light switch, we won't be seen."

Kate and Daisy followed the beam of light, settling on a mound of soft loose hay.

Finn switched off the flashlight.

"Can you leave it on?" Kate asked. "It's so dark. We'd hear someone coming ... wouldn't we? Then you could turn it off."

"I think so. Gee, this is just like summer camp when I was a kid. All the boys and girls told scary stories around the campfire, each trying to tell a story scarier than the last. It was fun."

"I don't think this is fun," Kate said. "Do you really think this is fun?"

"Well, as I see it, someone is playing a big joke on Louie. Whoever that is, he saw the house today, a dollhouse, and decided it was an opportunity for a news story. I bet the culprit leaks the theft to a TV station in the morning. The police search around Lakeville and find us in this old barn.

"You have to admit it's a cute story especially when they show a picture of my tiny house and Big Red. Who knows, maybe it was Cameron's idea for a publicity stunt."

Chapter 34

———

THE SWEET SCENT OF hay mingled with the musty humid air. The barn, closed off from the world, turned into a sweat tank, making it difficult to breathe. Finn waved the flashlight around the cavernous barn, and then with a deep sigh, he handed it to Kate. "Here, hold this while I call Georgie."

" ... "

"Georgie, Georgie, wakeup. It's me ... Finn. Are you there?"

"What? Huh? I'm here. It's almost midnight. Why the heck are you calling me?"

"Kate, Daisy, and I have been stolen," Finn said, punctuating each word.

"Finn, goodnight. I'm not in—"

"Wait, wait. Don't hang up. My cell is about to die and I need your help. We were in my house. We just laid down ... the mattress is really nice by the way ... and the house started to move. We've been kidnapped, but the robber didn't know we were in the house. Please call the police."

"Wow, that's terrible," Georgie said. "I think someone is playing a prank."

"Where are you?"

"I don't know where we are, twenty minutes or so down the road from the tavern. The guy turned left out of the driveway, sped down the road and then turned left again onto a bumpy dirt road. At least I think it's dirt. Then, get this, he drove right into a humongous barn. Honest to God, Georgie, it's the biggest barn I've ever seen."

"Finn, are you playing with me?"

"No, no. Just telling you. The police probably know the barn ... I've never seen anything like it. How did we miss this barn ... all those years we hiked around here?"

" ... "

"Georgie? Georgie?"

Finn looked at his phone's blank screen. "Kate, my cell's dead."

"Use mine ... darn."

"What's the matter?"

"I forgot my purse. Hold the light for me—"

"No, you stay here. Tell me where it is. I'll get it. Give me the flashlight."

"The loft, beside my pillow," Kate said in a loud whisper, looking over the edge of the hay bale at Finn scampering down the ladder.

Shuffling to the front door, Finn hoisted himself up on the porch. A few seconds later there was a flash of light through the little window in the loft, then again on the porch. Finn jumped down, his knees buckling as he dropped the flashlight. Regaining his footing, he hustled up the ladder to Kate and Daisy.

Catching his breath, he flopped down next to Kate, handing over her purse. "No point calling Georgie again. Save your battery," he said switching off the flashlight. "Let's just wait. Georgie got most of the message. He'll get us out. What was it you wanted to tell me if we got out alive."

"We aren't exactly all the way out, Finn." She stuffed her cell in her purse, and began rocking back and forth with Daisy in her arms.

He sensed she was having trouble breathing in the heat. "I know, but while we wait for Georgie—"

"I ... I was just thinking ... maybe the robber is after me."

"Why?"

Kate didn't answer.

Finn heard her breathing spike. She was gasping for air. "What's the matter, Katie? Tell me." He reached for her hand ... her hand was shaking. "You can tell me, babe," he whispered.

He waited for her to speak. She was breathing deep through her mouth.

"About six months ago ... Daisy and I saw a murder. Finn ... I'm afraid ... I'm sure he's after me ... after Daisy and me. I think he found us."

"Wait. Who was murdered and why would he be after you and Daisy?" Finn's demeanor instantly changed from fun and games to dead serious. What was Kate telling him? She was really scared and Daisy, the chatterbox, wasn't saying a word.

"Daisy and I were in the house when my ... when my sister screamed. Then ... there was a gunshot. I'm sorry I told you a lie. Daisy isn't my daughter. She's my niece. I'm not really—"

"Aunt Kate, I want you to be my mommy." Daisy began to cry, snuggling into Kate's arms. "Please ... can I still call you Mommy?"

Rocking Daisy faster, Kate tried to comfort her. "Shh, sweet girl, of course you can call me Mommy if you want to ... for now."

Finn slid closer to Kate, touching her arm holding the child. "What happened after you heard the gunshot? Did you see your sister ... you know ... dead?"

"Yes, as Daisy and I passed the living room to the kitchen, to get out of the house. Karen was on the floor in front of the fireplace ... she was laying on her back ... the fireplace poker beside her ... but that wasn't what killed her. Oh God ... her eyes were staring at me." Kate was struggling for air, gulping, her body trembling.

"Karen's your sister?"

"Yes." The word was more of a choke as she struggled to stay in control.

Finn held her closer, stroked her hair. "Was she bleeding?"

"She was shot in the forehead. Blood was everywhere ... pools of blood everywhere." Kate's voice strangled as she rocked Daisy, tears streaming down their cheeks.

Finn felt Kate's tears on his hand as he held both of them, wishing he could block out the scene in their minds.

"Did you see who—"

"Not exactly. But I heard his voice?" Kate was trying to stifle her tears as Finn wiped her face with his handkerchief.

Clinging to her aunt, he heard Daisy whimper. Finn felt for her face, wiping her tears away, too.

"Who was it?" Finn whispered, barely able to get the words out of his mouth, but words that had to be spoken.

"It was Smitty, my sister's second husband, Daisy's stepfather. He wanted my sister's money, money she inherited from her first husband's estate. He was a realtor … he died in a terrible car crash when Daisy was two. Karen married Smitty … on the rebound. I'm sure he just wanted her money. They had terrible fights, constantly quarreling over money. I heard them quarreling that night. He was demanding she put him in her will. He said that because he was her husband he was entitled to be named in her will … if anything happened to her. She yelled back that she would never include him … and then yelled that she was going to change her old will cutting him out entirely so it would be clear he was to receive nothing … yelling that she wanted a divorce … shouting that she wanted him to leave the house. That's when I heard her scream."

Finn tucked Kate's head under his chin, his hand splayed on her hair holding her to him, wondering how he could comfort her.

"But … if you heard his voice then—"

"I grabbed Daisy, our coats, my purse and my sister's shoulder bag off the kitchen counter. Smitty was calling to us … demanding we come to him. We ran out the back door, got in my car and drove off. "I cleaned out her bank account the next morning before we caught a bus. That's what we've been living on. I didn't care where the bus was going. I bought tickets for the first bus leaving the city. We were the last passengers to board. We might have ended up in California, but it was heading east."

"Where in Wisconsin are you from?"

"Madison." Kate stopped rocking her niece, tears continuing to stream down her cheeks, her body convulsing with fear and at the same time relief at finally revealing her story. "I'm sorry ... I didn't mean to cry ... it's just ..."

Finn rocked them both. *Think. Think.* "You should go to the police. Explain—"

Kate jerked out of his arms. "I can't. Smitty knows Daisy and I were in the house. He knows we heard him kill Karen. When I drove off, he tried to follow us but I kept turning and finally lost him. We stayed in the car until the bank opened. I ditched my car several blocks from the bus station. Two days later in ... I don't know where we were ... at a bus station, I picked up a newspaper. There was a headline about a real estate heiress being murdered in her home. It was my sister. The article said her husband was brought in for questioning but he had an alibi. Finn, he got a woman to lie. She swore Smitty was with her."

Tears sprang again, Kate gulped for air. "But get this, the article in the newspaper stated that Smitty fingered me for the murder. The police let him go and I became the prime suspect. They said I was the one after my sister's money. They're building a case against me ... I'm sure of it. Daisy and I ran and ran so he couldn't find us."

Daisy whimpered again as Kate patted her back.

"So, that's why I think the hijacker is after us. Smitty found us. We are the only ones who know he killed Karen. He wants to eliminate us, kill us."

The dank air in the barn had turned sinister. Words—a scream, a gunshot, murder—suspended in the air.

Chapter 35

———

IT WAS ALMOST MIDNIGHT. Shadows skipped around the tavern from the flickering flames of the candles remaining on the bar. Louie was alone. Kate and Daisy were in Finn's house.

Louie paced from the grill, to the backroom, back to the grill. His pudgy hands held up in surrender.

"What am I gonna do? What am I gonna do? Scarface means business. He's gonna come back."

Louie's eyes darted to the front door hearing the creaky hinge. A man stood in the doorway, his hand gripping the old handle on the tavern's front door. Sauntering in, his eyes squinted, darting around, fixed on Louie.

Terrified it was Scarface, but seeing it wasn't as the man emerged from the shadows, he let his hands hang down to his side. "Sorry, mister, we're closed," Louie said. "Darn latch didn't catch. I'm cleaning up," he said, taking deep breaths trying to steady himself. "I can get you a beer before—"

"I'm not looking for a drink. I know it's late, but I'm looking for someone. I was told she might be in the area."

"No strangers moved in around here. Of course, there are lots of bikers who stop off before heading up to the mountains, or back home. Unless she's a biker woman, there's no new woman moved here to Lakeville, none that I know of, anyway."

"You see, she and I had a falling out. She took off with our kid. Left in the middle of the night. A little quarrel and she ups and leaves. Women … hard to figure them out. I guess I will have that beer, if you don't mind."

Relieved that Scarface hadn't strolled in, Louie sauntered behind the bar. "Bottle okay?"

"Sure. Anything cold."

Louie uncapped the first bottle he saw in the cooler, setting it in front of the stranger.

"As I said, no woman—"

The stranger pulled out a photo from his back pants pocket, laying it on the bar. "Here's her picture. Ever seen her?"

Louie looked at the picture, turned away, throwing the bottle cap in the trash. "Nope. Never seen her. What makes you think she's in Lakeville?"

"She charged some groceries nearby."

"As I said, I've never seen her. Enjoy that beer," Louie said, handing the picture back.

Ambling around the end of the bar to the grill, he pretended to scrub the surface with a steel pad. Runaway wife? Not Kate with little Daisy. No. But maybe I should warn her someone is asking, is flashing her picture around. Maybe she's in trouble.

Louie sauntered to the backroom, shutting the door. Warn her. She's sleeping in the little house. I could go knock on the door, but I'd probably scare her to death. I'll call. She'll see it's me.

Louie pulled his cell from his pants pocket and punched Kate's cell number stored in his directory.

His call went to voicemail.

"Hi, Kate. Louie here. Probably nothing, but I wanted to let you know that a man just came in. He was looking for his runaway wife and kid … his exact words. Thing is, he showed me a picture of his wife. It was your picture. Bye."

Louie hustled back to the grill.

"Want another beer, mister?"

"Nah. This is good. I'll be leaving soon as I finish. Tastes pretty good. It's been a long day."

Louie looked up, looked out through the grill window, as the creaky tavern door opened again. His legs buckling, he grabbed the edge of the grill to keep from falling.

Scarface sauntered up to the bar. "Missing something, Louie?" he hissed.

"No, no. I'm not missing anything," Louie said with a stutter.

"Well, maybe you should take a look ... like out back."

"Why, why ...

"Just take a look. I'll follow you. Go look."

The stranger sitting at the other end of the bar followed in line. Louie led the way, opening the back door.

The tiny house was gone.

He stood gaping at the empty stand of trees. Kate and Daisy were inside. His eyes darted to the left. Georgie's car was gone. Georgie had dropped Daisy off and left. Finn either went with him, or was he inside the house with Kate and Daisy?

Louie whirled around, his eyes wide with terror.

"That's right, Bulldog. Your new trailer park is empty. Now, why don't you step inside, and you and I will have a little chat."

The stranger leaned against the door leading to the backroom watching the action pinging back and forth between the two men in front of him. If he was a betting man, he'd say that the fat little cook, fear gripping his body, had something the man with a deep scar on his face wanted. And, whatever it was, the man with the scar was willing to inflict considerable pain to get it.

Chapter 36

THE BARN WAS STIFLING with no breeze to move the heavy air building from the day's heat. In spite of the heat, Daisy fell into a deep sleep, her chin drooping as she snuggled in Kate's arms.

Kate's story took over Finn's mind, blotting out any plans to escape the predicament he found himself in. There were so many questions he wanted to ask her but feared it was too painful for her to relive the murder of her sister. *Maybe it was an accident— hitting her head on the stone fireplace. The fireplace poker on the floor next to her head was damning. Could have been an intruder hit her with the poker when she screamed, then shot her. But Kate seemed so sure it was her sister's husband she heard.*

"Finn, Finn. Hear that?" Kate whispered, snapping Finn out of his thoughts.

Finn cocked his head. "Sounds like a fire engine. Maybe they're looking for us. Let's get out of here. We can wave them down."

"Okay. Wait ... there's another siren."

"That's a police car. Come on ...

"Wait, I left my tote on Daisy's side of the mattress ... my wallet's in it," she said.

Muffled sounds of a fire engine approaching filled the barn, grew louder, then receded, followed by more sirens. Police?

"They're coming for us. Come on, I'll carry Daisy down the ladder, you follow me," Finn said, reaching out for Daisy's hand, scrambling down the ladder.

At the bottom, Kate clutched Daisy to her. "They're not coming for us, Finn. They went passed, in the direction of the tavern."

"All the more reason to scram before the guy comes back, checks the house. Oh, oh. Wait."

"What did you forget?"

"Louie's briefcase. He'll kill me if I lose—"

"Really, Finn? A briefcase?"

"Well, it's just as important as your wallet. That's the way he would see it. I'll be right back."

"Don't forget my tote ... by the side of the mattress?"

"I'll get it. Wait here."

Kate watched the beam of light. He flicked it twice in the loft window. Another few minutes and the beam was on the porch, then the ground as Finn fixed the light on Kate and Daisy waiting by the ladder.

"Now can we get out of here? Looks like another slider at the far end. I'll carry Daisy. You hang onto my shirt. I don't want the flashlight on when I open the door. No telling who's on the outside. Look, there's a door beside the slider. Let's try it."

Finn pushed through, stepping out of the black hole into the moonlight.

"I don't see anyone. Do you?" Finn asked.

Kate twisted her head glancing around. "No."

"See those bushes ahead ... we'll walk fast, hide behind them."

"Finn, look ... that orange glow. Looks like flames. A fire."

From behind the corner of the bushes, Finn stopped. The woods were passable but thick with underbrush. Thinking about Kate's story ... did he believe it? Unfortunately, he tended to believe her, which meant he had to get help.

"You and Daisy stay here. I'll go for help. We can't chance going to the street in case the guy comes back, especially with a fire in the area. I can make better time by myself, but don't move. You'll get lost."

"You're probably right. Daisy and I will stay right here, but be careful."

"I will." Finn leaned over, kissed Daisy's cheek. "You take care of your ... mommy." Then he grasped Kate's cheeks, planting a burning kiss on her lips. "I'll be back, babe ... soon. Remember, stay right here."

Kate nodded. Within seconds Finn vanished into the thicket of bushes blanketing the forest floor.

———

"LET'S SIT ON THE LEAVES, Daisy, so no one can see us."

"I don't like it here, Mommy. It's scary."

"I know, but Finn will be back soon. We can sit by that tree, look up at the stars. Everything is going to be fine."

Leaning back against the tree trunk, Daisy leaning against her arm, Kate retrieved her cell from her purse, thinking that it would be a good idea to tell Georgie that she and Daisy are in the bushes behind the barn.

The cell blinked.

There was a new message.

Kate tapped the message at the top of the list.

> "Hi, Kate. Louie here. Probably nothing, but I wanted to let you know that a man just came in. He was looking for his runaway wife and kid ... his exact words. Thing is, he showed me a picture of his wife. It was your picture. Bye."

Fear coursed through Kate's body. Smitty had found them.

"Come on, Daisy, up you get. We have to get out of here," Kate said, stuffing her phone in the tote.

"But you told Finn—"

"Things have changed. Give me your hand."

Kate ran down the dirt road, ran down to the street. Gripping Daisy's hand, her tote swung from her shoulder on the other side. Daisy's little legs ran as fast as they could trying to keep up, but she stumbled. Kate quickly helped the little girl back up. Standing behind a bush next to the shoulder of the road, she hung back, holding Daisy behind her.

She watched. Waited.

A car went by, another car. Then she saw the lights of a semi-trailer truck.

Stepping out of the bushes into the truck's oncoming lights, she began waving.

The truck slowed to a stop, leaving the engine running. The driver pushed the button to open the window on the passenger's side.

"You got to be more careful, lady. I might have hit you if I wasn't paying attention."

"My car broke down. Can you give me and my daughter a lift?"

"Sure, hop in."

"Thanks, mister." Kate lifted Daisy up to the cab, the driver pulling her onto the seat, then stretched out his hand to Kate. "Thanks, I'm in," she said, pulling the heavy truck door shut.

"Fasten the seatbelt around the two of you, lady."

"Yes, sir."

The truck lurched forward, gaining speed in the direction of the tavern.

A policeman was standing by the tavern's driveway. He waved the truck on. Kate and Daisy, looking out the truck's window, saw the tavern was on fire, an inferno. Firemen were spraying water on the flames trying to bring the blaze under control.

"Where were you and your daughter going at this time of night?" the driver asked.

"Where are you going?"

"Hartford, Connecticut. There's a truck stop I like—shower, and shave—just in time for breakfast."

"That's wonderful. My parents live in Hartford. That's where we were going."

"What about your car?"

"I'll call … I'll call to have it towed to the nearest gas station. My dad will take care of it."

Daisy fell asleep in her lap and Kate turned her face to the window, head tilted against the headrest, pretending to be asleep. *I wonder if Finn's okay. What's he going to do when he realizes we're gone? We had to leave. With Smitty so close, I'd put him in danger … all the Bradley family. At the truck stop maybe Daisy and I can catch another bus. I don't care where it's going. We have to get as far away as possible from Bradley Farm.*

Chapter 37

———

FLAMES SHOT HIGH INTO the sky torching nearby pine trees. Billowing smoke pushed westward on the summer breeze. Sirens continued to pierce the hot, humid, July air, as more and more fire engines answered the call to help contain the spreading blaze.

Finn continued his struggle through the thick underbrush, determined to find help for Kate and Daisy. He could feel the heat of the flames when the breeze washed over his face. By his calculations, the tavern couldn't be much further.

The top of a pine tree a few yards in front of him suddenly burst into flame.

"What was I thinking?" he muttered. "I can't leave Katie and Daisy to face ... God knows what."

Hesitating, seeing Katie and Daisy in his mind huddling in the dry leaves, he turned, began retracing his steps—each step, each swipe at a branch more urgent than the last. Glancing up he couldn't see the weathervane on top of the giant barn imprisoning his house. Gathering clouds and smoke blocked the moonlight.

"Katie! Katie!" he shouted.

He stood still a moment, listening for her to call out to him. There was no answer. "I have to be close. Where are you?" His words sounded hollow.

He hadn't been in this area of the forest before.

Maybe he was confused.

Maybe he was going in circles.

Standing on a wedge of granite, his eyes frantically searched the sky again for the weathervane.

"There, there it is," he muttered.

Veering slightly to the left, he picked up his fight with the underbrush, forging ahead, keeping the weathervane as his compass.

"Kate! Katie! Daisy!" he yelled. "Where are you? Yell if you hear me."

Finn broke through the underbrush just as a pair of high beams flashed up the dirt road. He stood frozen in the oncoming headlights. A line of police cars followed, circling the barn.

The lead car screeched to a stop. Georgie jumped out. He ran to Finn, pulling him into a fierce hug.

Finn whirled away, ran back into the bushes shouting. "Kate! Kate! Daisy!"

Georgie followed on his heels.

"I left them here. Right here. Right here," Finn said turning left, right, left again. "Georgie, where are they? Did you see them on the road? Did you see them beside the road?" He was gulping for air, fear rising in his belly.

"No. I'm sorry, Finn. I didn't see anyone on the road. Are you sure this is where you left them? It's so dark."

"Kate! Kate!" Finn called again, his voice weaker as it became obvious Kate and Daisy were not where he left them. Bile rose in his throat at the thought they might be caught in the advancing flames. "Georgie, give me your phone. Mine's dead." Fumbling, Finn tried her cell but it went right to voicemail. "Kate, where are you? Please, please call me."

"Come on, Finn. They're not here. They must have gone for help. Maybe she was afraid of the approaching fire. It will be daylight in a few hours. We'll get a search party together. Gran and Jane can start checking with the neighbors. You can charge your phone."

"She doesn't know the area. She could be lost in the woods. Georgie, I can't leave her." He raised his hands forming a cone around his mouth. "Kate," he yelled. Cocking his head in vain, listening for her reply.

Finn looked over his shoulder. The flames had died down. Only dense smoke lived on, now licking at his nostrils. "What if she got confused and tried to move away from the fire, but instead moved closer. I told you, she doesn't know the woods. Georgie, I have to keep looking," he said, as he tried her cell again. Voicemail.

A police officer stepped out of the barn. "Nobody in the barn. Where are the other two?" the officer yelled as he approached Finn. It was Tommy Townsend, the tight end on Finn's high school football team. Finn had seen him a couple of weekends ago at the tavern.

Finn shook his head. "I don't know." He turned to go back in the woods but Georgie grabbed his arm. "Come on, Finn, we have to wait for daylight. They probably got turned around, lost their bearings in the woods."

Finn, restrained by Georgie's grip, stopped. Staring into the woods, the thick brush in the black night, he knew Georgie was right. Without turning, he asked Georgie, "Where's the fire?"

"The tavern. It's gutted. Nothing but the shell is left. Whoever stole your house did you a favor by getting it out of there," Tommy said.

"Anyone hurt?"

"A fireman found a body."

Finn turned around, faced Tommy silhouetted in the moonlight. "Who?" the words, trapped in his throat, came out in a faint whisper.

"Louie. He's dead."

Finn's head dropped.

Georgie's hand slid off of Finn's arm.

Tommy stared at his friend. "He was shot in the head."

Chapter 38

———

THE GRAY LIGHT OF dawn crept across the night sky as Georgie turned up the driveway where a few hours earlier he found Finn. He stopped to the side of a scowling man standing at the edge of the grass, hands on his hips. He knew the man to be a third generation of the Scarpetti family. He also knew there was bad blood between the Scarpetti family and the Bradley clan. Scarpetti was not distracted by the car that stopped beside him. At the moment he was nose to nose with Detective Tommy Townsend.

Finn jumped out of the car, muscled his way between Tommy and Scarpetti, fists balled to punch the elder Scarpetti. "Where is she? Where's Kate and her little girl?"

Scarpetti didn't back down a hair. "As I told Detective Townsend, I don't know what you're talking about. I don't know any Kate, or a little girl. Search the house if you want. Are you the owner of that rusty truck attached to a cockamamie dollhouse in my barn?" he said snapping each word through clenched teeth.

"Your barn? Since when?"

"Since two weeks ago."

"You bought this house? I never saw a for sale sign on the road?"

"Private sale. You know the old adage—stay close to your friends and even closer to your enemies … something like that."

Finn looked over his shoulder at the barn. The barn doors were pushed open wide, showing the burnished glow of his house's cedar siding as the morning sun breached the horizon.

"Yep. That's my house that you stole last night." Finn turned back to Scarpetti.

Scarpetti jabbed Finn in the chest.

"No, you punk. I didn't steal your rusty truck and I certainly wouldn't have a need for the toy house. And, I want you to get it out of my barn … now!"

"I sure will, right after I search the woods around *your* barn. Tommy, why don't you search his house. Let me know if you find anything." Glowering at Scarpetti, Finn shoved the man aside and jogged off to the thick bushes where only a few hours ago he had kissed Kate and Daisy, telling them not to move, that he would be back with help.

Stepping into the bushes, he stopped short. Was that his cell? *Could it be Katie?* Fumbling, he pulled the phone out of his pants pocket.

"Finn, Cameron here. Carrie and I are calling about your brewery. We'd like—"

"I can't talk," Finn snapped, slapping his phone shut.

Blind fear filled Finn's eyes, afraid of what he was going to find in the bushes. Side by side he and Georgie forced their way through the underbrush, rotting trees lying on the ground, a clear patch now and again. Circling back to where they began the search, they locked eyes. There was no trace of Kate and Daisy.

Finn dropped to his knees, hands on his head, despair in his eyes. He was a beaten man. "Why do you have to lose someone before you realize how much they mean to you?"

"You haven't lost Kate. We're going to find her," Georgie said, squatting on the ground about three feet away. He was struggling to lift something lodged in a large bush. "Look at this," George said, wrenching a briefcase free of the brambles.

Finn watched him set the case on the ground.

"It's Louie's … was Louie's. So this proves that this is where I left Kate and Daisy. I threw it in that bush when I left for help."

"If it's Louie's, why did you have it?"

"Louie was afraid of something, or someone. He told me to hide it, but if anything happened to him, it was mine. I stashed it in my house, but I brought it with me when Kate and Daisy and I left the barn."

"It's a beautiful briefcase. Expensive leather. I wonder what's in it."

"I don't know. You can open it when we get back to the farm. Right now I want to talk to Tommy. I'd like to hear more about Louie being shot. It scares me, Georgie. Louie shot ... Kate missing. I want to know what the police can do to find Kate. I'm afraid she and Daisy have been kidnapped. She's in danger ... just as she feared."

Chapter 39

———

TOWNSEND STARED AT SCARPETTI, the pair standing outside, waiting for Finn to finish searching the brush behind the barn. Trouble was brewing between Finn and Scarpetti. Detective Townsend had seen it before with the Boston-based mob family. Punches coming out of nowhere and Townsend didn't have a backup. Georgie would step beside Finn leaving Townsend to untangle the men.

The detective was strong but he didn't like the odds. The minute he arrived at the house, Townsend knew something was bothering Scarpetti, and he was right. While the detective was searching the house for Kate and her daughter, Scarpetti followed him like a rabid skunk. The man volunteered to the detective that his son, Logan Scarpetti, hadn't returned home last night. His son was an angry man with a deep scar on his face and the elder Scarpetti was afraid he'd gotten into a brawl again.

Tommy stepped in front of Scarpetti. He looked at the open barn doors and then back at Finn, emerging from the woods. He carried a briefcase, but no sight of Kate. "Take your truck and house back to the farm," Townsend said to Finn. "I have to stay, talk to Scarpetti, get his statement. I'll stop at the farm after I check in at the station, and after I see what else the officers found at the burned out tavern."

Georgie slid open the back barn door so Finn could pull straight out. No need to back up, which was tricky with the house on the trailer. There was plenty of grass for him to make a wide turn, then a straight shot down the dirt road to the street.

Finn climbed up behind the wheel, his face grim. "Where's Kate, Georgie? Where's Daisy?"

Georgie could only shake his head. He didn't know and couldn't even venture a guess. "When Tommy stops by to see you at the farm, ask him what he can do to search for her—call in other officers … I don't know, Finn. Let me out. I'll walk back and get my car. I'm sure Scarpetti won't want it on his property even for an hour. I'll catch you back at the farm, bro."

———

FINN STOOD IN THE SHOWER, the steamy water beating down on his body. He leaned forward, hands on the wall under the showerhead, going over and over again, his last moments with Katie.

The kiss.

Did he miss something? Was there a sign in her body language that indicated she was going to run?

Shaking his head, he turned off the water, slid down the wall, sitting, watching the water drain. There was no sign of a struggle in the bushes, not that there would be with all the leaves. If she left with someone, she must have known who it was. But surely she would have had a chance to call me. Call the farm.

Standing, he grabbed a towel. Drying off, he stared in the mirror. *What am I missing?*

Where was he going to even start his search, and oh, mark his words, he was going to search and he would find her. In his heart, he believed she cared for him, and there was no doubt in his mind that he loved her more than life itself.

Pulling on his jeans, he finished dressing to join the family in the kitchen. The scent of sausage roiled his stomach, but he could use a cup of coffee. Maybe with Pop's help, the two of them could come up with a plan.

———

"YOU HAVE TO EAT something, Finn," Gran said. "How about a muffin warmed with butter in the skillet to go with that coffee?"

"Sure, Gran. That would be nice. Thanks—"

"A squad car is coming up the drive," Jane said, looking out the window. She stood at the sink rinsing the breakfast dishes.

The squad car parked by the back door as Finn rushed out. Detective Tommy Townsend climbed out of the car and faced his friend. "Nothing on Kate but I did stop by the tavern, what's left of it. Let's go inside and I'll tell you what the officers found."

"Hello, Tommy. Can I get you a cup of coffee?" Jane asked.

"No thanks, Mrs. Bradley. I won't be here long. Good morning, Mr. Bradley, Georgie. Nice to see you again, Wolfe." Nodding in turn, they all waited patiently for the detective's report.

Tommy turned to Finn. "The old, dry-wood ceiling throughout the tavern burned, fell along with most of the beams. Some of the charred beams are still smoldering. The officers found three bodies in the ashes. Louie Tuttle, Scarface-otherwise known as Logan Scarpetti, and a John Doe. Louie and Scarface both died of gunshot wounds. One of the officers speculated that John Doe died of smoke inhalation. From where his body was found, it appeared he was trapped by the grill when a beam fell on him."

"Who do you think he is ... this John Doe?" Finn asked. He was standing with hands on the back of a kitchen chair to steady himself.

"We don't know. Two guns were found, one by Scarface and one by John Doe. They've been sent over to ballistics. Officers are sifting through the ashes around Louie and Scarface to find the bullet casings so we can reconstruct what went down at the crime scene."

"Tommy, stay a minute. I'm going to call Marshall—all this gun stuff, and with Kate missing. Kate told me a crazy story while we were hiding in the barn. I want you to hear it. Maybe Marshall will have some ideas on how to find her."

Gran started a large pot of coffee to brew while Finn called his brother. Marshall answered on the first ring.

"Hey, little brother. What's up?"

"I need your help, Marsh. I'm in the kitchen at the farm—the phone's on speaker. Tommy Townsend is here. Remember him? I don't know if you've seen him since he became a police officer. He's here because my truck and house were stolen ... and the tavern burned down ... and two people were shot dead ... and a third died from the smoke and—"

"Hold on, Finn. Not so fast. The three bodies, have they been identified?"

"Two have—Louie, my boss at the tavern, and a guy called Scarface. The third one ... we don't know who he is. I'll explain all that after Tommy leaves—everything has to be verified as to what and how it happened. But first ... you met Kate and her daughter Daisy?" Finn stopped pacing, staring at the phone on the table.

"Yes. Fourth of July. Very cute, both of them. Go on."

"Kate's missing and so is Daisy?"

"Missing?"

"Yes, wait, wait. I want to tell you the story she told me just before she went missing."

Georgie set mugs of coffee on the table as Gran poured.

"Whoever stole my truck and house didn't know that Kate, Daisy and I were in the house. He parked the truck with the house in a huge barn. I didn't know where we were, but thought we should get out of the house. So we hid in the barn's hayloft. I called Georgie telling him my truck and house were hijacked, and that I didn't know where we were. My best guess was twenty or so minutes from the tavern."

Finn, his hand shaking, took a sip of coffee, nodding thanks to Gran.

"The three of us were sitting in the hayloft and Kate tells me this crazy story, like a confession. She said Daisy isn't her daughter, she's her niece. She said maybe the hijacker was after her. She said, back in Wisconsin, she was at her sister's when she heard her sister scream and what she thought was a gunshot. Kate grabbed Daisy and took off in her car. She was positive her sister's second husband shot her. She said Smitty, that's the husband's name, wanted the sister's money."

Finn paused, taking a breath, sipping his coffee.

"Sorry, Marsh, it may seem like I'm rambling but honest to God this is what she said. Anyway, on the way out … sorry I didn't get the order right … Kate saw her sister on the floor. Her sister was shot in the forehead and there was lots of blood. She and Daisy have been missing ever since. I have to find them, Marsh. Please, please help me."

Finn collapsed on the chair. Everyone in the kitchen looked at the phone then over at Finn.

"Sit tight, Finn. I'll text Sadie and Travis in Washington. Travis can find out about this Smitty person. I'll leave for the farm now … I should be there in a couple of hours. In the meantime, jot down everything you can remember, exactly what Kate told you so you don't forget anything. I want you to repeat it to me again. Did she say when this murder took place?"

"Yes, six months ago. Madison, Wisconsin."

"What about her sister's name … last names—sister, and this Smitty?"

"She only referred to them as Karen and Smitty."

"Okay. Tommy, let Finn know what has to be done to put a trace out on Kate. Finn, do you have any idea where she is?" Marshall asked.

"No, I told her I was going for help and to stay put. By that time we were out of the barn and hiding in the bushes. Hang on. Tommy wants to talk to you."

"Marshall, I don't know what went down here last night, but it was bad. I still have nothing on Kate and Daisy. Seems they disappeared in thin air. Finn will give me a call when you get here. I'm heading back to the station to put out an All Points Bulletin on Kate." Tommy turned to Finn. "Do you have a picture of Kate and Daisy?"

"Yes, on my phone. When we finish the call I'll print a couple of copies ... whatever you need."

"And give me a description of what they were wearing," Tommy said.

"Ah, Kate had on a pair of jeans, white blouse ... and white sneakers. Daisy wore a pair of flowered capris, little yellow and white daisies, and a green T-shirt. I don't remember anything about her shoes."

"Finn, print a couple of pictures for me and Travis, too. Tommy, the Scarface guy, is that Logan Scarpetti?" Marshall asked.

"Yes. Mr. Scarpetti senior, the third I believe, bought a house down the road. It was his barn where we found Finn's house and truck. I don't know what will happen when I tell Scarpetti his son was shot dead."

Chapter 40

———

TENSION FILLED THE AIR as the Bradley family coalesced around their wounded family member. There was no doubt about it— Finn was suffering a deep wound. Calls between Marshall, Travis and Finn burned up the airwaves every half hour with the latest information. By mid-afternoon, Travis asked for a conference call to bring the family up to date after his last conversation with Captain Krueger, Criminal Investigation Department, Madison, Wisconsin. The Lakeville case was handed over to the captain as soon as the Madison police chief received the call from Detective Townsend.

The family had gathered around the kitchen's harvest table waiting for Travis to call, to hear the details of what he learned since this morning. Travis had spent the time digging for more information from Captain Krueger.

The farmhouse landline was set to speaker phone when Travis placed the conference call. Sadie was by his side in the Washington D.C. condo they shared.

"Everybody ready?" Travis asked.

"Everyone except Detective Townsend," Marshall said. "He's stuck at an accident scene on Route 95—a semi-trailer truck overturned near Portsmouth. Wolfe and Georgie are here along with—"

"What did you find out … about Kate?" Finn asked, cutting Marshall off. Unable to sit still, he sprang from his chair, paced to the sink, fingers gripping the porcelain, as he looked out the window to the barn and his tiny house. He fervently wished he could turn back the clock to when he and Kate and Daisy, were happy inside.

"There's an open murder case in Madison that occurred February eighteenth," Travis said. His tone serious but soft, aware that he was giving information that was going to rock the family listening over five-hundred miles to the north.

"The crime occurred in a house on the outskirts of town. The owner of record is one Karen Smits, formerly Karen Cutler, maiden name Karen O'Leary. Karen Smits was found dead the morning of February nineteenth by the cleaning lady."

"Karen O'Leary? That has to be Kate's sister," Finn said, stepping from the sink, his hands grasping the back of his chair at the table, his eyes fixed on the phone centered on the table.

The backdoor bell rang, sending Lucas into a frenzy. Finn rushed to the door, motioning Tommy to come in. "Hold on Travis. Detective Townsend just came in. Repeat what you found … the name sequence … Karen Smits," Finn said, lifting the pup into his arms, stroking his silky head trying to quiet him.

Travis heard the chairs shuffling as he repeated the information. "… yes, Karen O'Leary and Kathleen O'Leary are sisters. They grew up in the Wisconsin foster-home system. And get this," Travis continued. "Karen Smits is married to Carl Smits who goes by the nickname of Smitty."

Tommy leaned forward. "Hi, Travis. I'm Detective Townsend, Finn's high school friend … Tommy. He's told me about you. Did you get a chance to ask the CID Captain in Madison how he wants to handle a possible identification of the body we have in the morgue? From what Finn says, Kate was sure her sister's husband was after her … fearing she could put him at the murder scene. Just maybe he found her here in Lakeville. Anyway, it's the only possibility as to our John Doe's identity. Oh, and then there's a gun we think was John Doe's. It was found near his hand." Townsend said.

"Yes. Krueger said to send a DNA sample of the body. Overnight it, if you can. Send him the serial number on the gun along with the DNA kit. He'll check the registration. It could be a break in his case if it's registered to Carl Smits. Text me the best way to reach you, Tommy, and I'll do the same back to you with Krueger's address for the DNA sample. Please keep me in the loop."

"Right away." Tommy stood. "We haven't had any luck with the APB on Kathleen O'Leary—"

"We need to find her before the police in Madison do," Marshall said, as he stood, paced to the kitchen window alongside Finn who again stood at the window his head bent down.

Finn whirled around. "We have to find her, Travis. Give her a chance to defend herself. No way she could kill anyone and never her sister. She's protected her sister's child," Finn said breathing fast, trying to hold his emotions together. "She's not Daisy's mother. She's her aunt. She's—"

"You're right about finding her first, Finn," Travis said. "Townsend how about Finn going on television? National television. Sadie, can you pull it off with your contact in Boston?"

"I'm sure of it. If we give them an exclusive as the case evolves," Sadie said. "First broadcast—no names. A personal interest story about a missing woman wrongfully accused of murdering her sister. If Kate sees the broadcast—"

"Oh, my God, Travis. It's just as Katie said. She's sure this Smitty person killed her sister, and—"

"He has an airtight alibi. But, Finn—"

"He can't have an alibi, he—"

Travis cut him off. "Finn, there's a warrant posted nationwide for the arrest of Kathleen O'Leary for the murder of her sister. They believe she's armed and dangerous. She could be shot if she tries to run from an officer."

"Oh my God, Travis, I have an APB out on her," Tommy said.

Travis sighed. "So do the police in Madison."

Chapter 41

———

KATE WAS ON THE RUN!

A warrant was out to arrest Kathleen O'Leary for the murder of her sister!

Worse yet, she might be killed fleeing, because officers were warned that she was armed and dangerous.

The mood around the kitchen table was grave. The magnitude of what the arrest warrant meant throbbing in everyone's head.

"Well, I don't believe a word of it," Jeli said, her voice soft, lacking conviction.

Gran and Jane sat, hands folded in their laps, eyes scanning the family. Everyone was struggling with the mounting evidence against Kate. How could the pretty woman they met on the fourth of July be a murderer?

Georgie pushed his chair back, the legs scraping the floor like nails on a chalk board, his eyes seeking his dad's. Wolfe looked up, raising his brows. What was his son going to do?

Georgie hustled out of the kitchen. There was nothing more to be done until Townsend, Travis and Sadie started to execute their side of the investigation. He returned a few seconds later with Louie's briefcase, setting the case in front of Finn.

"Okay, Finn, let's see what Louie was hiding. Time to open this beast. Maybe it holds a clue as to what happened at the tavern before it burned to the ground."

Sighing, Finn turned the luggage-size briefcase to see the keyhole. Retrieving his keychain from his front pants pocket, he fingered the gold key Louie had pushed in his hand, and turned it in the lock. Everyone sitting around the table stepped behind Finn, looking over his shoulders.

Finn lifted the lid of the case. A folded piece of yellow paper lay on top of a red and white checkered dishtowel covering the contents of the case. Setting the yellow sheet aside on the table, he lifted the towel.

Jaws dropped.

Two rolls of gold coins were wrapped in a zip-lock bag. No one, except Finn, knew what they were looking at.

"Bitcoins. Louie's bitcoins," Finn whispered, his finger caressing the clear plastic bag.

"Surely they aren't real gold … are they?" Wolfe asked.

"No, they're brass. Louie showed me once, not long ago. He explained them to me. Bitcoins are a currency created in 2009, if I remember correctly, by an unknown person using an alias. You can make transactions without a middle man—meaning, no banks. There are no transaction fees, and you don't need to give your real name. You can buy all kinds of things—big, small, expensive, cheap. Louie said some people buy bitcoins as an investment hoping that they'll go up in value, which is what Louie did.

"I remember him pacing around in his apartment above the tavern. He said bitcoins became the world's biggest cryptocurrency. Cryptocurrency is digital money—not a physical currency. Louie said the first investors bought a coin for five cents which gradually increased over the first two or three years to five dollars per bitcoin. How about that for a rate of return? But then Louie got very excited telling me that in 2013, the value jumped as high as a thousand dollars per coin, even more, but dropped to around five hundred dollars. Boom to bust with no FID insurance. It was very risky. If the virtual place storing your virtual money loses it all, you're screwed."

Finn unzipped the bag, handing a coin to each person around the table. "These are Casascius bitcoins. I only know that because Louie told me. Embedded in each coin is an address, and a code. Logging into his accounts, Louie had access to the amount of money represented by each coin, the equivalent amount of dollars. Late 2013, Casascius suspended the sale of physical coins that contained the address to the virtual coin, or, put another way, the digital bitcoins. Physical coins are still minted but they aren't embedded with the address of the account. People buy them as gifts, souvenirs, by opening an account and buying a virtual bitcoin equivalent with real money from their bank account. You don't buy or sell anything with a physical bitcoin, only virtual coins."

Finn fingered one of the coins, his mind wandering back to the day Louie told him about the coin he now held in his fingers. "Louie told me the history of bitcoins, said I should know because maybe one day he'd give me a couple," Finn said with long sigh.

"These coins were minted before 2013, so if you look at the back of them, you can see the hologram with its own bitcoin address and the amount the coin represents. It's redeemable with the private key inside, underneath the hologram. You can't tell by looking at the back of these coins what the value is—I'd have to access the account online."

"If you're telling us, these coins are equivalent to real money … can you access it?" Pops asked.

"I'm not sure," Finn said.

Beside the plastic bag was a thick, steno-size tablet. The cover of the tablet was folded back, held in place with a rubber band. Line after line of what appeared to be account numbers filled the top sheet, each line ending with a dollar amount. Finn picked up the tablet revealing several file folders, some bulging with sheets of paper.

Opening the first folder he thumbed through the stack of printout sheets. He glanced at the tabs of the other folders and then set all of them back in the case. "Pops, in answer to your question, can I access the money … I think so. Looks like Louie kept a list of his accounts, the addresses, and the codes, along with the value each coin represents. Each coin is equivalent to a different amount, the amount of dollars he paid for it."

"How much is all this worth?" Gran asked, her index finger tracing the back of the coin in her hand.

"It fluctuates, Gran. But when Louie first showed me the coins, several months ago, one bitcoin was worth $240."

"So, it looks like there are … maybe twenty or so coins here," Georgie said. "You just inherited about $4800?"

"Not quite. Remember, each physical coin in this case represents an account. The tablet, with the rubber band, lists the accounts and the dollar value in each account … at the time Louie last checked. So the total value, of the bitcoins, in this bag is more in the area of five-hundred-thousand dollars," Finn said, picking up the folded yellow piece of paper.

"Son, are you jerking my chain?" Pops said, bug eyed.

"That's the way Louie explained it to me."

Jeli reached for the plastic bag, dropping her coin inside, and passed it to her mom, who added her coin. The bag was passed around to the others, and then set in front of Finn.

"Strange, one of the folders is labeled *Scarface*. Let's see what Louie has to say about him." Finn retrieved the Scarface folder from the bottom of the case. There was only one sheet in the folder, handwritten. Finn scanned the sheet and then read the words aloud.

———

"HOW I, LOUIE TUTTLE, came to own my tavern.

Many years ago, my parents, now deceased, gave me fifteen thousand dollars to pay for my first year in college. Unbeknownst to them I opened an account on an online poker site. I was excited. Here was a grand new adventure.

I went to college but quit after a year, and never took a job with a company. I played poker—sometimes I won, sometimes I lost, but I managed to keep paying the rent of my dinky apartment.

But then along came bitcoins and I invested in the beginning of this new currency and made bunches of money on my investment.

I kept playing poker, learned I was good at it, literally turning my college money into a down payment on a bar, now my tavern, the Cock and Feathers. My parents were furious, practically disowned me when I told them what I'd been doing over the years. They thought the idea of a tavern ridiculous. They died soon after and I paid off the tavern, and turned most of the rest of my inheritance into bitcoins, hoping the currency would appreciate more. And it did—big time.

About a year ago I had a visitor. The visitor introduced himself as Mr. Scarpetti, but said to call him Scarface. Said everyone did. I accepted it because he had a deep scar down his left cheek—ear to chin. He said he looked me up when he saw my profile on the poker website. We were practically neighbors he said. I came to realize that he was a mob member of the Scarpetti family, well known in New York and Boston.

Scarface accused me of cheating at poker, cheating him out of thousands of dollars and he wanted me to pony up. He said he would accept payment in bitcoins. He had filed a complaint to the online poker site. They froze my account until they investigated the claim against me. There had been a few irregularities when he and I were part of the same virtual poker table. The poker website officials, after their investigation, found nothing that could be proved. But, Scarface didn't believe them and still claims I owe him. I don't owe him a nickel. I learned, too late, never to fill out an internet profile with my real name or address.

His demands became worse when he learned my tavern was located near Bradley Farm, a few miles down the road from my tavern. The Scarpetti family still believes that Bradley Farm holds the key to thousands of dollars worth of items stolen from the mob decades ago.

I continue to have run-ins with Scarface.

And, so it goes. Scarface accusing me of cheating, me swearing I didn't.

Louie Tuttle"

———

FINN RETURNED THE SHEET to the Scarface folder, setting it back in the case. Leaning back in his chair, he looked up at the ceiling, seeing the little man he had worked beside, a man who was always kind to him, and now he was dead. Bending his head down, he stared at the case that Louie had given him to protect.

"What's on the yellow paper," Georgie asked.

Finn sighed and picked up the folded yellow paper that was on top of the towel when he opened the case. He scanned the writing, sat bolt upright, scanned it again and began reading out loud.

———

"Louie Tuttle – My Will

Let all know that I, Louie Tuttle, being of sound mind, declare this to be my last will and testament. I have no other will, never got around to it.

This briefcase contains two rolls of bitcoins, the value of which is held in my online accounts. The access codes and passwords for the accounts are listed on the enclosed tablet. Backup information is on the printout sheets in the folders enclosed in this case. Also enclosed is the background of the false allegation by Logan Scarpetti, otherwise known as Scarface, that he has a right to these coins. He does not.

In the event of my death, I leave the bitcoins and my tavern, Cock & Feathers, and the land it stands on to Finn Bradley, hoping that one day his dream of a brewpub will come into being. So, as I wrote above, this being my last will and testament, I leave everything I own to Finn Bradley.

Louie Tuttle"

———

FINN SHOOK HIS HEAD, a tear sliding down his cheek. "It's signed the day of the fire. Like he knew he was going to die. He was afraid of Scarface … he came to the tavern that day … knocked Louie around. Maybe that's what prompted him to write his will that day. He had to have written it just before he gave me the briefcase to hide. I hid it immediately under the loft mattress in my house … the same day my house was stolen." Finn looked up, brows drawn together in pain, his chest rising and falling rapidly. *The same day Kate went missing. The same day my world fell apart.*

"But he didn't give you the deed before he died," Wolfe said.

"I think he did." Finn drew a deep breath, withdrawing a folder labeled *Tavern Documents*.

Lucas got up from under the table, stretching front and back. The only sound in the room was the pup scratching his ear.

The ring of the phone lying on the table startled everyone. Finn punched the speaker button. "Hello."

"Finn … are you there?" It was Sadie.

"Yes. We're all here. Haven't moved," he said wiping his eyes with his handkerchief.

"The television spot is all set for tomorrow." Sadie's voice was strong, in control.

"Wow sis. That was quick. What time tomorrow?"

"Eight in the morning. Traffic will be brutal into Boston at that hour, so I suggest you leave no later than six. You can grab breakfast at a café near the station.

"I'm flying up tonight … staying with Marshall. I'll text you all the info—the station address, where to park, etcetera. Oh, and Finn, be yourself—cowboy hat and all. The network understands the urgency. They look at it as a human interest story—you and Kate."

Chapter 42

———

GLASS WALLS LINED THE long hallway, dividing each side into offices. On the north side the office windows looked out over the Charles River, the southern exposure was filled with the city skyline and Boston's financial district. Finn and Georgie followed the willowy blonde down the hallway to an open door. She waved them into a conference room. A long mahogany table dwarfed the space. Maroon leather chairs on casters, slid under each side of the table, two on either end. The exposure—southern.

"Have a seat, gentlemen. Sadie Bradley will be right … here she is now," the blonde said with a broad smile.

Finn hardly recognized the woman in the black suit, her thick black hair pulled back in a French twist. Sadie, on the other hand, didn't miss a beat throwing her arms around her brother. She quickly switched, giving Georgie a hug as she whispered in his ear. "Thanks for coming with him."

Sadie stepped back to her brother, grasping his shoulders. "Finn, listen to me. We are going to find Kate. Now, come sit down. We'll go over how the taping works."

Sadie took a seat at the head of the table, signaling Finn to sit around the corner facing her. Georgie took a seat on the opposite side. He'd never seen Sadie in action and was amazed at how professionally she handled the situation.

"You will have a sixty-second spot," Sadie said, keeping eye contact with Finn, exuding support for her brother. "The final cut will air immediately and then at the top of the hour, every news cycle, every hour on the hour, as well as tomorrow morning. Did you jot down what you want to say?"

"Yes, but I need your opinion on how—"

"Just be yourself."

"That's what you said on the phone. Are you sure? I put a jacket in the car," he said, fumbling with his hat.

"You're perfect. I want Kate to see you—hat and all—not a stiff stand-in. You have to convince her not to be afraid to call you, that you will protect her. When you look into the camera, visualize Kate. Speak directly to her. The cameramen will shoot one practice take so you get the timing. I will introduce you, then it's your turn to talk, and then back to me asking anyone with information to call the number at the bottom of their screen. Did you bring a picture of Kate?"

"Yes, right here. Georgie printed it out for me." His fingers were shaking as he opened the file folder he carried in a leather binder that his mom used for important papers. "Pop's gave me a frame, if you think—"

"No frame. The picture is perfect. Georgie, thanks for cropping out Daisy. We can filter crank calls from people who don't know about her little girl."

Sadie leaned forward, squeezing Finn's forearm.

"Alright, everyone. It's show time." Sadie stood up, held out her hand to her brother, then walked him down the hall to the studio, her arm casually through his arm. "You look wonderful. Thanks for taking my advice in dressing like you always do—cute cowboy hat, plaid shirt, and jeans. Remember, you're talking to Kate, reassuring her she will be safe if she calls you."

The group walked into the studio ablaze with floodlights, camera equipment, and a table with two chairs in front of a dark-blue wall. Georgie hung back as Sadie guided Finn to the table, nodding for him to take a seat as she sat beside him.

The run through was rough. Finn looked nervous, stumbling on his words. Sadie hoped the practice session would help settle him once he knew what to expect. Of course, she knew the crew would have to cut the tape down to less than sixty seconds, so she was confident her brother could handle it.

"Okay, Finn. Let's give it our best shot."

Finn nodded. His heart was pounding, but he did what Sadie suggested. Suddenly he was looking into Katie's beautiful blue eyes. He wanted to reach out, hold her, tell her how much ...."

"My name is Sadie Bradley. My brother and I need your help to find a missing person, a person who is very close to him. Here is my brother, Finn Bradley."

"Katie, I miss you, I will keep you safe. No one will hurt you. If you can hear me, if you can see me, please call me."

The camera switched to Sadie holding up Kate's picture, the camera zooming in full screen. "If you have seen this woman, if you have any information on how we can contact her, please call the number at the bottom of the screen. My brother and I thank you."

———

"YOU DID GOOD, FINN," Sadie said, giving him a fierce hug. "Let's hope we get a call. Come on you two, I sent for some sandwiches and coffee in the conference room. We'll have a bite and then I have to scram to the airport, catch my flight back to Washington."

"Thanks, sis. I just pray someone calls."

Finn and Georgie followed Sadie back to the conference room. Just as they sat down, their blonde escort rapped on the door and entered. "Miss Bradley. A call just came in on the tip line. A man. He asked for you."

"Transfer the call in here, please."

Finn stared at the phone on the conference room table waiting for the call to be transferred. Sadie snatched the receiver on the first ring.

"Miss Bradley here. You called the tip line?"

"Yes, ma'am. I was eating breakfast at a café, saw you and your brother on television. I think I saw the woman in the picture you showed except she had a little girl with her. You didn't mention a—"

"That's right we didn't, Mr. ... what's your name?"

"Stan. The woman in the picture flagged me down on the road. It was late and very dark. I told her she had to be more careful. I could have hit her. She asked if I could give her a ride that her car broke down. Before I knew it she had lifted the little girl up into my cab and was climbing up beside her. I asked where she'd like me to drop her off. She said she was going to see her parents and then asked me where I was headed. I told her Hartford, Connecticut, a truck stop. She said that would be fine, she'd call about her car from there."

"Did you pass a fire after you picked her up?" Finn asked.

"Oh, yes. A big blaze. An officer waved me through."

"Did Kate, that's the woman's name, did she say anything?" Finn asked.

"No, she didn't. Just pressed her forehead to the window, watched over her shoulder as we went by. She turned the little girl toward me ... I guess so she wouldn't be scared by the fire."

"Did you drive to Hartford ... the truck stop?" Sadie asked.

"I did. I helped them down out of my rig. She thanked me, and walked toward the truck stop's restaurant. I went the other way to grab a shower."

"Did you see them after that?" Finn asked.

"Nope. When I got to the restaurant she was gone."

"Thank you, Stan. Thank you for calling. You've been a big help. Do you mind giving me your number, you know, in case we have a question?" Sadie said.

After writing down the number Sadie hung up the phone, she looked at Finn with raised brows. "That was fast."

"Yes, it was fast, but we don't know much more than we did before. Only that she and Daisy got a ride to Hartford. We don't know what spooked her in the first place, and worse, we don't know where she's going," Finn said, twisting his hands around his handkerchief, drying the sweat from his palms.

Chapter 43

———

"I HATE YOU," DAISY SCREAMED.

The little girl sat cross legged on the motel bed. Her hands balled into fists pounding the flowered quilt, tears cascading down her red face. "You're not my mommy."

"I know I'm not your mommy. I'm like your second mommy. Your real mommy loved you very much and I love you very much. I'm trying to keep you safe, both of us safe." Kate, tears erupting from her eyes, sat cross legged at the foot of the bed facing Daisy. "

"I want to go back to Finn. He's my friend. I want Lucas. Finn gave him to me. You took me away from my dog."

"I'm sorry," Kate whispered, crawling off the bed. She padded on bare feet to the bathroom, dousing a washcloth with cold water, and returned to Daisy. "Here, dry your eyes. We have to get something to eat. We're both hungry. The café across the street looked nice … a burger? Peanut butter and jelly sandwich?"

"I'm not hungry. I don't want to eat ever again."

"I'm not leaving you here alone. If you don't want to eat, you still have to come with me. We'll bring something back to the room. Come on." Kate took the washcloth from Daisy, and wiped her own eyes. Hoisting her shoulder bag, she felt in the bottom for the small cylinder of mace she bought in New Hampshire. That was before she met Finn at the tavern. After meeting him, the fear that Smitty would find her diminished. She let her guard down. A big mistake.

"Come on, Daisy," Kate said, slipping on her sneakers.

Daisy reluctantly climbed off the bed but refused Kate's hand. She didn't want to be left alone, but she wasn't ready to make nice either.

Kate didn't know where they were headed only that she wanted to get as far away as possible from New Hampshire. When the bus from Hartford stopped in New York City, they got off and went into the terminal. She decided to switch buses to make it difficult for Smitty to track her. She purchased two tickets to Philadelphia, an adult and a child but they missed the bus by minutes. The next one didn't leave until four in the morning. When she spotted the blinking motel sign across the street from the bus station, she thought it might be a good idea to rest. But with Daisy's meltdown, she wished she'd asked for another bus, one that was leaving immediately.

Kate was starving and hoped that Daisy would change her mind and eat something. Crossing with the light, she paused at the alley beside the café, putting the bus tickets in the pocket of her tote. A man came up from behind, reaching out to snatch her tote. He tried again, but Kate was too fast for him, whirling around, hitting him in the head with the black canvas bag. Daisy began kicking the man as he stumbled backward falling against the brick wall of the alley. Kate grabbed Daisy's hand, dragging her along as she ran into the café.

The cashier was startled by the woman and child charging in the door, falling against the checkout counter. "Are you all right? What's—"

Shaking, Kate tried to catch her breath. "A man ... tried to steal my bag ... in the alley ... just now—"

"Go over to that booth. I'll call the cops. They'll—"

"No, no. He was probably hungry. We just want a couple of peanut butter and jelly sandwiches. Our bus ... our bus is leaving."

"Okay, hon. I'll get your sandwiches and then I'm going to report it. We can't have our patrons mugged."

"Hurry, please, our bus is about to leave."

"Sure, sure, hon. They're already packaged. That'll be $8.30. Would you like something to drink?" The lady stopped. Kate threw a ten-dollar bill on the counter and darted out the door with her child.

"Hurry, Daisy. Hurry." Kate pulled the little girl across the street, up the sidewalk to the motel. Fumbling with the key, she opened the door, pushing Daisy inside, slamming the door behind them."

––––

THE BUS HISSED AS the driver slowed to a stop at the Philadelphia terminal. Stepping off the bus, stretching, Kate took Daisy's hand. The little girl was too tired to protest. In the terminal, Kate looked at the various destinations. The next bus was to Arlington, Virginia.

It wasn't leaving for an hour. It was two o'clock in the afternoon, so she decided to take Daisy across the street to a coffee shop rather than a sandwich from the machine in the terminal. Traffic was heavy, foot traffic even more so. Kate liked the feel of blending in with the crowd. She was still shaky from the attack in the alley the previous evening and she was almost out of cash.

A policeman sitting at the end of the counter kept looking over at her. When he retrieved his cell from his shirt pocket, tapped a number, Kate left money on the table and hurried out of the shop with Daisy in tow.

The officer had turned to the wall to talk, away from the person sitting on the stool next to him. When he turned back, the woman and the little girl were gone.

Within minutes Kate and Daisy were sitting in the back of the bus as it pulled out of the terminal on its way to the next stop, Arlington, Virginia.

Chapter 44

———

OTHER THAN THE TRUCK driver, nothing substantive had come from Finn's plea on television. He wondered if he was ever going to see Kate again.

Leaning against the frame of the back door, a piece of straw between his teeth, Finn's eyes automatically fixed on his tiny house, imagining Kate inside chatting with Daisy. Without them the house had lost its glow. *Home is where the heart is,* he thought, and his heart was breaking. Lucas sat against his master, his paw on his shoe. The pup uttered a soft bark, looking up at Finn. Finn bent down, picking up the pup, stroking his curly fur. "I hear you, Lucas. I miss them too," he mumbled.

Stepping back into the kitchen, everyone, except Sadie and Travis, were gathered around the table. Jeli, in the middle of a sentence, closed her mouth when Finn walked in. "Talking about me, Jeli-bean?"

"Just thinking out loud. Seems like all we can do is wait. I'm not very patient."

Gran sat in her rocking chair, a pillow behind her back. The ladder-back chairs at the table were uncomfortable so, when there was a gathering, other than mealtime, Georgie carried her rocker in from the living room, positioning it near the head of the table so she was included in the circle.

Gran cleared her throat, breaking the silence permeating the room. At family gatherings, she preferred to hear what everyone else had to say on this or that. But not this time. Tapping her foot on the floor, her chair moved in an easy rock. Her voice was strong.

"Bradley farm has seen many changes. The first Bradley, Marshall Bradley, bought the land, built the house, and started a dairy farm. It stayed a dairy farm for a few generations until my husband's father, Mason Bradley. None of you knew him. Anyway, Arnie's father sold all but a couple of cows and began raising horses. Arnie followed his father's passion for horses, except he took that passion several steps further. My husband liked the track, not betting mind you unless it was on one of his horses. He began breeding racehorses. Remember Sir Charles, Danny? Sir Charles was his prize stallion and won numerous races resulting in soaring stud fees.

"During the horse years, the land became virtually fallow. Our one remaining cow grazed, the horses trotted around newly fenced corrals, but these endeavors didn't take up even a quarter of the two hundred acres.

"When Arnie died suddenly of a heart attack, the horse business died with him. Danny was away serving our country when Arnie died. He and Jane were newlyweds, and their twins were on the way. You all know about Danny's war injury. He was in no condition to take on the heavy lifting a farm requires. I was certain we were going to lose the farm…"

Gran's foot tapped harder, the rocker picking up speed.

"… bringing me to the heart of my ramblings. None of the Bradleys produced more than one child. I may be wrong there by one, but no more. We're not quite sure about Marshall Bradley. Those initial years are a bit murky. So, while I was sure the farm was going under, two things happened … at the same time. Jane went to college, business school, spending hours on her studies—spreadsheets she called them … I used a journal, pen on paper … but not Jane. She was on the computer pumping out those spreadsheets.

"She was full of ideas on how to transform the farm, once again. She called them business centers. Her ideas seemed radical to me. I wasn't keen on Jane when Danny announced that he was going to marry a city girl. I was wrong ... very wrong. Best thing you ever did, Danny, marrying this city girl. She showed me a thing or two." Jane leaned over, patting Gran's hand. Gran grasped her hand squeezing it tight.

"Anjelica, you have one foot off the farm, and the other tethered to your room upstairs. But I have a feeling it won't be long before you're going to go the way of your big sister. You have so much creative talent ... well, I'll just leave it at that. Your mom and pops and I have had many a lively discussion on where your talents will lead you.

"The second blessing happened when one day, about the same time when Danny fell in love with Jane. A man called Wolfe strode up our driveway carrying his four-month old son in a basket. He said he'd work to pay for some milk for his baby, if we could spare it. Wolfe and Georgie stayed on, became part of our family, now a growing family for the first time in years. Jane and Danny added twins and two babies after that—Finn and Anjelica." Gran smiled at her grandchildren in turn.

"As I see it, there is an ebb and a flow to a farm. Children come and they leave making their own way. Sadie, a crime reporter, will probably never live on the farm again, but her roots are here and she's ready at the slightest call to return and help when needed. Wolfe, Georgie and Finn are different. They love the farm—each in his own way. Oh, Finn, left for a few years, married a woman who never appreciated his passion for the farm or his ideas.

"So here we are today. The antique barn, or shop, whatever you want to call it, is slowing down. When Jane and Wolfe cleaned out that barn, the bank was knocking at our door demanding payment on three loans Arnie and I had taken out. There was enough old stuff in the attic of this house, and in the numerous barns and outbuildings, to help us over the hump for several years. And, of course, there were the pine trees Arnie had planted. A stand of Christmas trees. Another of Jane's profit centers. Next came a revamping of the horse barn into a plant stand of sorts with holiday decorations. While it's been a modest success, it still hasn't caught on.

"My Arnie would be thrilled with all the activity going on now in the house, in the barns, in the fields. Finn and Georgie, you two putting your heads together discussing the possibility of planting new crops—hops and barley. I have a feeling that the brewery will come to pass, and Georgie will be sitting up on his tractor tilling, planting, and harvesting the new crops.

"As I said, there's an ebb and flow to a farm—seasons, crops, sometimes a totally new direction such as switching from cows to horses. Jane's business centers. The antique shop has about run its course and what's popping up in its place? A brewery."

Gran paused her foot tapping, then began tapping again.

"Now, I come to the pretty woman and a little girl who captured our hearts. Kathleen fits here. A mate for you, Finn, and an addition to the farm with her energy and her love for preserving jams, and jellies she shared with me at our Fourth of July celebration. I could be mistaken, but I believe she could make a go of the gift shop adding her touch to the plants and herbs. She would be part of our family—a family she's never had.

"During her last visit, Kathleen told me how she and her sister survived one foster home after another. She said they were never abused, but were left to fend for themselves. She told me how they fought to stay together. She looked wistfully out over our land, saying how lucky, how wonderful it was that Finn grew up on this farm with the love of his family around him. Kathleen could no more kill her sister than a chicken could stop eating its grain."

Lucas jumped up on Gran's lap, laying his head between his paws, whining for attention. She patted his soft fur, clucking quietly to him. He had moped around since the day Daisy didn't show up for their morning romp. Gran was the only one he chose to cuddle up with, to let console him.

Gran's head snapped up, her eyes locking on Finn. "Finn, you have to find them. You have to bring Kathleen and Daisy back to

Bradley Farm. Oh, yes, I saw the spark between the two of you. We all did."

Gran's rocker slowed. Stopped. Her gnarled fingers fished around in her apron's deep pocket, pulling out a pack of thin cigars and a lighter.

Eyebrows shot up. Was Gran going to light the cigarillo?

She didn't keep them waiting. Flicking the lighter, touching the flame to the tip, she inhaled ... exhaling a small puff of smoke.

Danny reached for his mom's hand. "Since when did you starting smoking?"

"Since your father died," she replied, as the phone rang.

Anjelica quickly walked to pick up the wall phone. "Wait, Sadie. We're all here in the kitchen. Let me put you on speaker. Okay, go ahead. Say something."

"Travis just heard from Captain Krueger in Madison. An officer called to say he spotted the woman and child pictured on the arrest warrant that was sent out to the major police units in the country."

"Where?" Finn asked.

"In Philadelphia. Near a bus station. They were in a coffee shop. He placed a call to the police in Madison. During his call, he turned to relay their description but they were gone. So, all we know is that from Hartford she traveled to Philadelphia. Finn, we have to go on the air again. The Associated Press picked up the story that the top suspect in a murder case in Madison was seen in Philly. I will take the commuter flight to Boston early tomorrow morning. Can you meet me at the station around 8:30?"

"I'll be there ... me and Georgie."

Chapter 45

———

KATE STRUGGLED TO HOLD herself together. Every few minutes she fought off stomach spasms causing her body to tremble, her hands to shake. With two hours to wait for the bus out of Arlington, Virginia, to Atlanta, Georgia, she had time to buy Daisy and herself a change of clothes—new capris and shirts. There was no doubt in her mind that Finn had told someone what she was wearing if he was trying to find her. Thinking of him knotted her stomach. How stupid to let him wangle into her heart, letting her guard down, putting him in danger.

"Come on, Daisy. Let's go shopping. That will be fun don't you think?"

"I guess so. Can I have an ice cream?"

"For breakfast ... how about a bagel instead? The bus passed a Walmart a couple of blocks back. I'm sure they'll have something to satisfy your sweet tooth, baby girl," she said, forcing a smile on her face. Kate walked out of the bus terminal, hand in hand with Daisy. Four blocks away, they entered Walmart.

Passing through the women's section, Kate quickly picked up a pair of jeans, a black T-shirt, and a black ball cap, pausing only long enough to check the size. The young girl's department was next.

"Here, Daisy, how about these jeans, perfect size for you and they'll hold up until ... until we find a city we like. What do you think?"

"I guess. Can we get a bagel now?"

"You bet … maybe two."

Striding through electronics to the groceries, they passed by the televisions mounted along the back wall, all on the same channel. Kate caught a news alert out of the corner of her eye. The male reporter said something about Wisconsin and a murder suspect spotted in a Philadelphia bus terminal. Kate froze, turning Daisy away. Kate's picture splashed on the screen. Putting the ball cap on her head, pulling the bill down to her brows, she grabbed Daisy's hand and jogged to groceries. Picking up a sleeve of bagels, she half dragged Daisy to the cashier station.

Three people were ahead of her. Kate glanced at the other cashiers. There were lines at all of them. Robotic cashiers scanning, scanning, scanning bar codes.

"Mommy, I'm hungry. I can't run anymore."

Now only one person, thumbing through a magazine, stood in front of her.

"I know, sweetie. Hang on. We'll be out of here soon."

Kate didn't want to take off the ball cap but, of course, the cashier had to scan it.

She was next.

"Nice morning, isn't it?" Janet said.

"Yes, yes, very nice."

"This is a pretty shirt, little girl … matches your blue eyes."

Kate gave the lady a twenty, waited for her change, and with the ball cap pulled low, Daisy in tow, raced out of the store, the plastic Walmart bags banging against her thigh. They ran through the parking lot, then slowed to a fast walk back to the bus terminal.

"Wait a minute, Daisy. I have to stop. Catch my breath," Kate said bending over, shoving the bags with their clothes at Daisy.

"What's the matter, Mommy?"

"Nothing … I just need to … come on. We'll change in the terminal, then you can wash your hands and eat a bagel."

Hurrying down the street, Kate dropped Daisy's hand, wrapping her arms across her stomach.

"Hurry, Daisy, keep up. I think I'm going to be sick."

Pushing through the doors of the bus terminal, Kate turned to the women's restroom where they had freshened up earlier after getting off the bus.

"Wash your hands, Daisy and don't leave here without me."

Kate quickly stepped into a stall, leaned back against the door. *No, no.*

She couldn't stop it. Her stomach clenched, bringing her to her knees. She grasped the rim of the toilet and vomited, followed by round after round of dry heaves.

"Mommy, are you okay? Are you sick?" Daisy pushed open the stall door seeing Kate on her knees bent over the toilet. "Are you going to die? Please, Mommy, don't die. I'll be good. I promise."

Head bent down, breathing deep, Kate said, "No, I'm not going to die. I have a stomachache. The worst is over. Can you get me a paper towel? Put some water on it if you can reach it."

Daisy dropped the Walmart bags and ran to the sink, to a woman washing her hands.

"Excuse me, lady, excuse me. My mommy is sick. Can you put some water on a paper towel, please?"

"Of course, honey. Here you go. Can I help your mommy?"

"No, thank you. Mommy said the worst is over. We're catching a bus in a few minutes."

The woman followed Daisy to the stall, looked in as Daisy pushed through. "Are you okay, miss?"

"Yes, thanks ... a bout of morning sickness ... comes and goes."

"Tell me about it. Looks like you're in good hands with your little helper."

Chapter 46

―――

THE HUMIDITY IN BOSTON was oppressive. Within minutes the back of a man's shirt, or the back of a woman's tank top, clung to their bodies with sweat. Office workers hurtled from one air conditioned building to another, from air conditioned offices to air conditioned restaurants.

However, the news bureau's studio was ice cold, even under the floodlights as they prepared for the taping.

Sadie sat beside Finn at the table in front of the dark blue wall—as before. She stepped through the sequence of the sixty-second taping scheduled to air throughout the day—as before. Sadie watched for the producer's signal to begin the broadcast which was different than before. This was live. The sixty-second spot would be spliced to thirty seconds to replay every hour.

"Hello. My name is Sadie Bradley. My brother Finn," Sadie laid her hand over Finn's hand, "is still searching for his friend Kate."

Finn stared ahead, the camera capturing the pain in his eyes, in the slump of his shoulders. The touch of Sadie's hand was the signal for him to speak.

"Katie, if you hear my voice, I ask you to call. If you fear for your safety, we can help. Call me. If someone is holding you against your will, I say to that person—let her go. She's done nothing to you ... I am personally offering a reward of thirty-thousand dollars to anyone who brings Katie and her daughter home to me ... Katie, please call me. I love you, baby," he said, a tear meandering down his cheek.

Sadie knew there was always a risk putting a loved one on the air live, but she was caught completely unprepared for what Finn had said. She could have the reward cut from all future spots but this one was out there for all to hear. The tip line was going to go bonkers.

Holding up Kate's picture, Sadie signed off. "Thank you, Finn. If anyone has information as to the whereabouts of this woman, please call the number at the bottom of your screen."

The floodlights were doused. A hush fell over the studio. The producer, pumping his fists, rushed up to Finn. Grinning, he looked from Finn to Sadie. "You may not have been expecting Finn to announce a reward, Sadie, but it made for great television."

"Shut up, Harry," Sadie said standing, waiting for Finn as he struggled to get up from the chair, the weight of the world pushing down on his shoulders. Sadie grasped his hand. "Come on ... into the conference room."

The blonde caught up with them as they were stepping down the hall. "Miss Bradley, a woman is on the line. She asked for Finn."

"Did she give her name?"

The blonde looked at Finn. "It's Kate."

Chapter 47

———

NOTHING OUT OF THE ORDINARY. A tranquil moment for the woman sitting in the bus terminal, her sleeping child laying her head on the mother's lap. Passengers passed her by without a second glance. However, at a closer look the mother appeared pale, her face drawn. The woman's eyes were filled with tears, as she stared at the huge television screen mounted above the rows of wooden benches. She was holding a cell phone to her ear, her other hand stroking her child's back. Her voice was mute.

The woman was Kate.

"Katie, are you there?" Finn whispered into the conference room telephone.

Sadie looked at Finn, motioning him to press the speaker button. He nodded, pushing the button. Kate's soft voice floated in the air cloaking Finn and his sister.

"Did you mean it? What you just said?" Kate whispered.

Her voice was so soft he could barely hear what she was saying. He leaned closer to the phone. "Babe, are you all right? Is someone holding you—"

"I'm all right. I just saw you on TV. Did you mean it? What you said … at the end?" she said, her voice fading.

"Kathleen O'Leary, I love you with all my heart. I've been so afraid something terrible happened to you. Are you sure you're okay? Is Daisy okay? Where are you?"

"I can't run anymore. We're so tired. I don't know what to do. The police are going to arrest me. What will happen to Daisy? I'm so tired."

"Baby, where are you?"

"… Arlington … the bus station. There's a pretty picture on the wall … tours at Mount Vernon. Imagine that. I wish I could take Daisy, but I'm too tired."

Sadie's cell was pressed to her ear. She was trying to talk to Travis but words were stuck in her throat, her eyes puddling. "Travis … Kate called. She's on the phone now. From what's she said we believe she's at the bus terminal in Arlington, Virginia. She described a sign for tours to Mount Vernon. She sounds traumatized. Wait, hold on."

"Sadie, I'm holding but I'm not waiting. I'm in the car. Twenty minutes. Tell Finn to keep her talking. I've seen this reaction before, someone running, hunkering down. They suddenly can't move and then just as suddenly they bolt. Finn has to convince her not to move, that I'm coming for her."

"Travis, you'll find them. I know you will. Call me as soon as you can. Let's assume you find them … take them to the airport. Finn, Georgie, and I will meet you at Logan Airport. You might be able to get a non-stop. Text me the flight number and time of arrival. We're still at the network in Boston. With any luck we won't have to wait long for you, but believe me, Finn won't mind waiting." Sadie looked at Finn. His eyes told her his hopes, his life, were resting on her shoulders. "Trav, call me. Let me know you have them. I love you."

Sadie touched Finn's hand. "Travis is on his way—no more than twenty minutes out of D.C." she whispered. "He says to keep her talking. Travis—"

"Sadie, she hung up."

Sadie stared at her brother. "You're sure?"

Finn nodded.

"Twenty minutes—Travis will be there." Taking a deep breath, Sadie grasped Finn's hand. "He'll find her, Finn. Travis will call the minute he finds her … we wait … he'll call."

As the producer expected, the tip line lit up but Kate's call was first. The network operator thanked the callers, taking their name, number, and details of the tip. While Kate had made contact, she was still on the run and the tips might still prove useful.

Chapter 48

———

TRAVIS STRODE INTO THE bus terminal, his eyes scanning the people milling around, scanning those seated. Kate and Daisy were not there.

Jogging through the open door to the bus platform, there were more people clustered in groups, waiting, others lined up at the hissing busses, the heavy fumes filling the humid air. The only bus loading was at Post 3.

Breaking into the line of passengers, he took the stairs in one leap. The driver looked askance. "Mister, get back in line. There's room. You don't—"

Travis flashed his FBI identification at the same time he saw her. Kate and Daisy huddled in the back. "Sorry, but I'm here to pick up a mother and her child," Travis said, already making his way down the aisle.

The driver, taking note of the ID, looked at the man dressed in a black suit and tie, white shirt, and shut his mouth.

Daisy was lying on the seat, her head in Kate's lap. Kate's head was resting on the back of the seat, eyes closed, arms and legs limp, toes of her sneakers pointing in on the floor of the bus.

Travis had to take it slow hoping Kate would recognize him and not start screaming. Approaching, he knelt in front of her, gently touched her hand.

"Kate … Finn sent me. You're safe … no more running."

Kate slowly lifted her eyelids as did Daisy.

"Travis?" Kate whispered.

Inwardly, Travis wanted to pull mother and child into his arms, reassuring them they were safe.

"Yes. Travis Drake. Do you remember me?"

"I'm tired, Travis. I can't run anymore. This is the last bus ..." Kate closed her eyes, her words trailing off.

Travis held his hand out to Daisy. The little girl was groggy but willing to let him lift her into his arms. With Daisy against his chest, Travis grasped Kate's hand, firmly bringing her to her feet. He kept his grip, as Kate shuffled along with him. Travis led her to the back door of the bus, down the steps to the platform.

Travis reached in his pants pocket for his cell. "Sadie, tell Finn I have them. We're heading to Reagan International. I'll text the flight info. And, Sadie, let's get married ... soon. I love you."

Chapter 49

———

THE HEAT AND HUMIDITY CONTINUED to rise as noon slipped into mid-day. Georgie was behind the wheel of the SUV, pulling into a parking space at Logan International Airport. He was glad Pops suggested taking his SUV. Driving back to the farm, no way he could have fit everyone comfortably in his car. The only people he wasn't sure of were Sadie and Travis. They might catch a return flight to Washington, but he doubted they would miss the reunion back at the farm.

Yup, Pops hit the nail on the head urging him to drive the big car to Boston. He was always concerned when Georgie was driving on the highway that his fifteen-year-old Chevy would break down.

Before they left the news bureau's conference room, Travis had called Sadie. He was at Reagan International Airport outside of DC. And was about to board a non-stop flight to Boston with an exhausted woman and an equally exhausted child with him. They were scheduled to land in less than two hours.

Sadie had a pass to the airline's private concierge service where passengers could rest, freshen up, while waiting for their flight or rendezvous with other passengers. Conversation consisted of few words—no, maybe, yes. They were still stunned by the miracle of Kate's call. Georgie and Finn were content to let Sadie take charge of the situation as she herded them to the VIP room. Now all they could do was wait. Sadie was lying on a couch, shoes off. Georgie was reading a magazine.

Finn's stomach was in knots. He had professed his love for Kate on national television, and again when she called. But she didn't say she loved him. *Maybe she just wants to stop running, be safe, and then ... and then what? Surely, she wouldn't go back to Wisconsin. Or, maybe she would.*

Finn couldn't sit still, pacing back and forth on the plush carpet. An attendant approached, asking him if he would like something to drink. He shook his head. *Thirty minutes and the plane should be landing. Probably preparing to land right now. Within minutes I'll hold Kate again. Hold Daisy's little hand.*

"Sadie, I'm going to the gate."

Sadie opened her eyes. "Finn, you can't go to the gate. The closest we can get is the baggage claim area." She slipped on her shoes and sprang to her feet. "I don't want to lose you. Come on Georgie, we'll go together."

Finn shot out of the VIP area, Georgie and Sadie in his wake. Following the signs, he jogged to Baggage, joining others waiting for a flight to land. He kept checking his watch as he paced at the bottom of the escalator, staring up at the passengers wrestling with their carry-on bags.

They must be deplaning by now. Where are they?

He saw Daisy first, then Kate, more beautiful than he remembered, his heart wrenching at how exhausted and pale she looked.

"Finn, Finn," Daisy screamed, running up to him, her little hands in the air inviting him to lift her into his arms. Finn caught her, hugged her tight, as Kate collapsed into his embrace, Finn's arms gathering the two of them in his arms, tears running down his face, streaming down Kate's face. Georgie pulled a handkerchief out of his pocket, handing it to Finn. Finn mopped Kate's tears, then his own.

Travis hustled up to Sadie giving her a warm hug and big smooch. She always loved his ardor when greeting her. She leaned back. "Good job, Agent Travis Drake."

"You, too. First time I've seen you a bit flustered in front of a camera."

Sadie looked at him quizzically. *Me flustered?*

Travis laughed. "I don't think you were expecting Finn to offer thirty-thousand as a reward."

"Well ... not exactly."

Georgie shook hands with Travis and then left to get Pop's car. Driving up to the arrival area, seeing more kissing going on, he gave three blasts on the horn as he pulled to the curb. Having their attention, he hopped out, opening the back doors for their sparse belongings as they climbed in the car. The silence of the previous two hours was gone, the air filled with quiet chatter, and then wound down, as Kate's head rested on Finn's shoulder, eyes closed, feeling the safety of his arms around her. Daisy soon closed her eyes, her blonde curls in his lap.

Speeding up I-95 from Boston to the farm, Finn's cell rang. He squirmed to retrieve the phone without waking Kate, whispering hello.

It was Tommy Townsend. "I have some news for you. Saw you on TV, Finn. That was something."

Kate raised her head, brows up, wondering who was on the phone.

"Hang on, Tommy, I'll put you on my phone's speaker. It's not that great so speak up. We're just leaving Boston with Kate and Daisy."

"Whoa. I wasn't expecting that. Are you going to the farm?"

"Yup. Should be there in an hour."

"I'll meet you there."

"What's your news, Tommy? You sound excited, so it can't be bad. If it is, wait 'til we see you, but if it's good, tell us now."

"Kate, can you hear me?" Tommy asked.

"Yes, but who are you?"

"Detective Townsend."

"Finn, no!" she whispered. "Is he going to arrest me? You said—"

"Trust me, babe. Tommy is an old friend. We've all been working to find you … and, he's working on the fire at the tavern. Something bad happened at the tavern the night you disappeared … I'll fill you in after we hear what Tommy has to say. He said it was good news. You're okay, Kate. Don't be afraid. Go ahead, Tommy."

"You'll be glad to hear this, I think. The third body in the tavern fire has been positively identified as Carl Smits."

"What? Oh, my God, Louie was right," Kate said, her hand on Finn's chest.

"Right about what, Katie?" Finn asked kissing her cheek.

"When you left me in the bushes, I got my cell out and there was a message from Louie. Wait, let me play it?" Kate reached in her jean's pocket for her phone. "Listen. 'Hi, Kate. Louie here. Probably nothing, but I wanted to let you know that a man just came in. He was looking for his runaway wife and kid … his exact words. Thing is he showed me a picture of his wife. It was your picture. Bye.'"

Finn laid his head back, eyes closed. "So that's why you ran. You knew Smitty was close … too close," he said in a whisper. "Did you hear that, Tommy?"

"Most of it. I want to hear it again when I see you at the farm."

Finn turned to Kate. Gently putting his hand under her chin, he turned her to face him. "It's over, Katie. No more running." *Now, if we can just get the arrest warrant set aside,* he thought.

Chapter 50

———

GEORGIE TURNED THE SUV into the driveway at Bradley Farm. "They're here," Jane called out from the kitchen window.

Gran was the first out the door followed by Jane, Pops, Jeli, Wolfe and Detective Townsend. Lining up in front of the flowerbed, Gran turned to the group. "Don't scare them," she snapped. "They have to be exhausted … but it is exciting," she added with a grin.

Georgie rolled the big black car to a stop in front of the welcoming committee. The minute Daisy climbed out of the car Lucas squeezed through the legs of the committee, dashing to the little girl. Giggling, Daisy and Lucas darted off to the goat pen to check on the baby goats.

Gran opened her arms wide to Kate who gladly stepped into her embrace. "Bless you, my dear. Welcome home."

One by one, the rest of the committee hugged Kate. Finn leaned against the car door watching the celebration, his heart full but apprehension lurking, growing, gripping inside his chest. She wasn't out of the woods yet. On the way from the airport to the farm, he had told Kate about Louie's death, and that Scarface had been found in the ruins of the tavern, both shot to death. The third body, now identified as Carl Smits, apparently died of smoke inhalation.

Arm in arm, everyone filed into the kitchen—a pot of coffee brewing and a plate of frosted cookies on the long table. They no more than sat down when the phone rang. It was Captain Krueger calling Detective Townsend and Finn. Finn pushed the speaker button, telling the captain who was present.

"Detective Townsend, did you tell Mr. Bradley that the DNA sample you sent matched a sample taken from the Smits' home, positively identifying your John Doe as Carl Smits?"

"Yes, sir. About an hour ago."

Kate squeezed her eyes shut, hearing the captain's words, verifying what Townsend had said.

Finn drew her into his arms. "Remember, babe, he can't hurt you … ever."

"There's more," Krueger said. "The gun found near Mr. Smits' hand was registered to him. When Detective Townsend and his officers reconstructed the crime scene, they found that the casings of the bullets that killed Louie and Logan Scarpetti came from different guns. The gun registered to Mr. Smits killed Logan Scarpetti. A bullet from a gun found in Mr. Logan Scarpetti's hand, was the gun that killed Louie Tuttle and fired the shots hitting a propane tank immediately causing an inferno. Scarpetti must have turned the gun on Mr. Smits who shot him. By then the fire was intense, trapping Smits when a beam from the ceiling fell across his chest."

Everyone in the kitchen sat mute, shaking their heads at what Krueger was saying. But Krueger didn't stop there. "The ballistics lab confirmed that the gun found in Carl Smits' possession was also the gun that killed Karen Smits. Carl Smits' alibi in the killing of Karen Smits evaporated. The two people who gave Smits the alibi recanted after hearing what had taken place in New Hampshire, and after I said I would not press charges against them if they came clean, admitted they lied about Smits being with them that night."

Krueger added that the lawyer for Karen Smits said her will named Kathleen O'Leary as Daisy's guardian, and left her considerable estate to her sister as well. "So Miss O'Leary, the warrant for your arrest has been nullified. Your sister's lawyer will be calling you. He needs you to return to Madison to handle your sister's estate, and I would like you to come to the department in the next seven days to give your statement of what you saw and heard the night your sister was killed, and to carry out your sister's wishes as stated in her will. I presume you can fly out?"

"Yes ... I'll call as soon as I can arrange it ... in the next few days," Kate said, wiping tears from her eyes.

"Captain Krueger, she needs a few days to rest up. Surely—"

"Finn, it's fine. A few days, Captain Krueger. I'll call."

"Good. I look forward to meeting you and your niece."

Chapter 51

———

WITH CAPTAIN KRUEGER'S REPORT, the marathon activity to find Kate the previous week, ended. Happy but exhausted, the family remained in the kitchen. Drained of all adrenalin pumping through their veins, they were unable to move.

Pops looked at Jane, who looked at Gran.

"Quite a turn of events, I'd say." Gran was sitting in her rocker, her foot tapping the floor. "Wolfe, I believe you told me you had a few bottles of Chianti in your wine cellar. Do you—"

Finn's cell rang. Fumbling, he pulled it out of his pocket, raising his brows to Kate. "Hi, Cameron, how are you?"

"Carrie and I saw you on TV this morning—"

Finn shook his head. "Hey, man, this morning seems like years ago—"

"You found Kate. It was just on the news. Arlington, I believe. We, Carrie and I are so happy for you," Cameron said, stutter stepping his words.

"Thanks, Cam."

"Finn …"

"Yes?"

"Finn … we … Carrie and I would like you to call us as soon as things settle down—"

"Go ahead, Cam. We're happy and relieved at this end, so consider this is me calling you. What's up?"

"Oh ... oh ... well ... Carrie and I have a proposal ... about the brewery. Would you consider taking on a partner?" Cameron rushed the last words, afraid if he didn't say them fast he wouldn't say them at all.

"Well, I—"

"Carrie and I want to invest in your dream. You see, it's been a dream of ours too, but we just couldn't come up with the courage to make it happen, and, well—"

"My God, Cam. Do you mean it?"

Finn grabbed Kate swinging her around as Daisy walked in from outside. Lucas wanted in on the swinging around fun, barking, jumping up on Finn's pant leg.

"Lucas, stop that," Daisy scolded. "Come back outside with me. It must be a new grownup game."

Smiling, Finn placed a quick peck on Kate's cheek, then looked at Georgie. "What do you think, Georgie? Sound good to you?"

Georgie nodded in agreement.

"Pops, Mom, your thoughts?"

"I think it's a splendid idea," Pops said, as Jane nodded her approval.

"Hang on, Cameron. The most important vote on the farm is Gran's. Well, Gran. Does this fit into the ebb and flow of Bradley Farm?"

Gran planted her hands firmly on the arms of her rocker and leaned forward, looking at the receiver on the table. "Cameron and Carrie Foster, your proposal to be a partner with my grandson is a capital idea. How soon can you get here?"

"Grandmother Bradley, this is Carrie. Cam will have to give a two-week notice, and so will I. We'll pack our tiny—"

"Gran, they have a tiny house, too, and—" Finn started to say.

"That settles it. You haul that tiny house of yours to the farm. I'm sure you'll find a lovely spot for it. Come as soon as you can, children."

Epilogue

Christmas Holidays

A DUSTING OF SNOW FELL over Bradley Farm earlier in the day creating a picture-perfect holiday painting. The months since Kate and Daisy were reunited with the family, and the arrival of Cameron and Carrie Foster in August spurred a frenzy of activities. Everyone pitched in on one day or the other, cleaning out the barn destined to be a brewpub. Construction was methodical, transforming the barn into a brewpub building, and then the installation of the fermentation tanks and equipment required for the brewing and bottling operation.

Finn and Cameron wanted the family's critical eye on what had been accomplished, along with a full explanation of what was planned, the list of projects still to be done to make the brewery a success from day one. The partners declared a respite over the holidays until January second, when they would commence the final push to open the brewery for business the first week in March.

Today excitement and anticipation were building—the brewery was ready for an audition of sorts, an unveiling showing the culmination of the work that had taken place over the previous months. Dinner was served in the kitchen beside the fireplace, a Yule log flickering gaily. Daisy and Jeli placed candles throughout the kitchen—countertops, mantel, and down the center of the harvest table. The little women, as Gran had taken to calling all the females now living on the farm, no matter their age, made quick work cooking the pot roasts and vegetables in three slow cookers. Now, only remnants of the juicy roasts remained.

Daisy couldn't sit still another minute. "Jeli, can we blow out the candles now? Can we, please? Finn, let's go down to the barn now, please, please."

"I second that," Travis said. "Sadie and I have seen some of the progress over the months, but I understand from Georgie that the fermentation tanks have been installed. I'm with you, Daisy, let's get this party started."

"Right on, Trav. Come on, folks. Cam and I have a barn to show you," Finn said, giving Kate a quick kiss.

"Shouldn't we clear the table first?" Kate and Carrie said in unison.

"Now now, you heard Daisy, no delay. Everyone, pick up your dishes, pass the sink on the way to the back door—last one out the door is a pokey turtle," Pops said, chuckling.

Closing the back door to the farmhouse, the Bradley clan bundled up in parkas, together with the new members of the household, strolled down the driveway to the repurposed tractor, thrasher barn reborn as a brewery.

Entering the barn, Finn flipped the light switch. To the surprise of everyone except Carrie, Kate, and Daisy, the barn came to life with tiny twinkling white lights strung along the bottom of the hayloft. Georgie had cut the last oversized pine tree from the area once alive with Christmas Trees. Another one of Jane's business centers now out of business.

The girls didn't have much time to decorate as they tried to shoo Finn and Cameron up to the house. The only adornments to the trees were strings of colored lights. Next year there would be more decorations, but for now they would make do with the lights.

Pops and Wolfe, on either side of Gran, Jane holding Pops other hand stopped short. "Well, I'll be," Gran said. "Who did all this?"

"We did, Gran. Carrie, Kate and I," Daisy said, bowing to Gran, then twirling like a butterfly. "Isn't it pretty?"

"It certainly is, dear. Very pretty."

It was the first time Sadie and Travis had seen the semicircular bar, the booths around the perimeter, and tables and chairs set in the expansive area, as well as in the loft. Daisy pulled Jeli to a table with two lighters. "Can you help me light the candles, Jeli?"

"Lead the way, missy."

On the other side of the bar was a glass wall, behind which stood the stainless steel fermentation tanks, gleaming in the overhead lights. Cameron, like a drum major, led the way to his area of expertise. Standing next to Sadie and Travis he explained the process of brewing the beer—how the liquid was piped from tank to tank. Cameron was waiting until after the holidays to begin testing the process. Pops and Wolfe had heard how the brewing worked several times when the tanks were installed so they sat at one of the pub tables swapping war stories that happened during the construction of the brewery.

Jane, Gran and Jeli joined the tour catching Cameron's excitement. Gran noticed Carrie hanging back, her eyes sparkling with pride listening to her husband, reveling in the fact that his dream was coming to fruition. Bradley Farm had provided an unbelievable opportunity for them. Wolfe and Georgie had already grown the first crop of hops and barley over the summer months and were talking about clearing more land. Georgie was researching how to provide cold storage to hold the crops until they were needed for the fermentation process.

"HEY, SIS, COME HERE. Grab a guitar. Let's play some foot-stomping tunes. Whatta ya say?" Finn called out.

"I say, bring it on, brother." Smiling, Sadie took the extra guitar Finn handed to her.

Strumming a few bars, they exchanged glances, then played a hot number, both singing. They quickly transitioned to a slow fox trot, following with a waltz.

Cameron swung Carrie into his arms. Pops, hearing a waltz, took Jane's hand, turning her into his arms, dancing to the slower tempo. Wolfe bowed to Gran, who straightened her spine and showed him a few steps of her own. Sitting out the next dance, Wolfe sought a new partner, lifting Daisy in the air, circling around, then resting her small feet on the toes of his big cowboy boots. Finn set his guitar down, nodding to Sadie to keep playing, as he swept Kate into his arms.

Love was in the air.

Returning to Sadie's side, the strumming reached a fever pitch as brother and sister began a playoff—one started a tune, followed by the other.

Jane felt a little fresh air would be nice. Putting her hand on Gran's arm, she leaned in. "Want to step outside for some air?" she whispered.

Gran caught the glint in her daughter-in-law's eyes. "Capital idea. Let's get our coats."

Bundled in heavy parkas, knitted scarves around their necks, Gran and Jane stepped out of the barn and into the starry night, a full moon beaming down. Finn had brushed the dusting of snow off the Adirondack chairs on the deck at the end of the brewery barn.

Settling in the deep wooden chairs, Gran reached in her coat pocket, pulling out a fresh pack of cigarillos. "Can I interest you in sharing a puff with me, my dear?" she said to Jane.

"I thought you might ask, so I bought a pack of my own."

"Tsk, tsk, I've lead you astray."

"Well, after you outed yourself the day Kate was found, I decided I'd get my own so we could have a tete-a-tete once in awhile. I couldn't let you puff alone, could I? But ordering up the blanket of stars is more than beautiful," Jane said, exhaling a small puff of smoke. "

"Anjelica told me she has an appointment next week in Boston ... with a developer. Or was it a builder? Same thing, I guess," Gran said.

"Yes. I hope it's the beginning of something. She's tried so many paths, but this one, interior design coupled with architectural design, seems to have really captured her imagination. At least, I hope so, and yet, that will mean she'll be leaving the farm. Maybe she'll commute for awhile. Still ..."

"Don't forget to wake me in the morning," Gran said, her mouth shaped in a circle as she released a puff. "I want to be at the top of the driveway when Finn leaves with his little house on the back of Danny's SUV. Imagine, all the way to Disney World."

"Finn promised Daisy, or she said he promised, to take her to meet Cinderella. Anyway, it will be a nice vacation for the three of them. They've been working so hard," Jane said. "When they come back he'll be faced with tons more work getting the brewery ready to open by spring. While Finn's gone, Cameron and Carrie plan to test the fermentation tanks. Carrie told Finn, Cameron would wait until he returned, but she whispered to me she didn't think Cam could wait. Cameron's tour was insightful wasn't it? Brewing is more involved than what I thought." Exhaling a puff, she looked up at the moon. "Finn and Cameron are a good match."

"I wonder what the first Marshall Bradley is thinking ... turning his dairy farm into a brewery—hops and barley instead of corn and hay for feed and bedding," Gran said letting a small puff of smoke escape her lips.

"Milking cows to brewing beer—quite a leap. Another new beginning for the farm," Jane said. "I just wish we could get the gift shop, and herb and flower gardens going. New blood will help with the addition of Cameron and Carrie. Putting down roots in their own tiny house on the lake near Wolfe's tree house, but not so close they lose the peace of the woods. I just wish Arnie was here to see it."

"The farm will thrive again with the new money—money which I don't profess to understand. Money that's real but I can't touch, or see—bitcoins. I declare, what is this world coming to?" Gran said.

"Gran, I bet you he's one of those stars, looking down with a grin on his face. The farm is like a city—comes to life at the dawn of each day. The seeds growing through the night while we sleep."

"Well, Jane dear, it's time for me to turn in. As I said, I want to wish Finn and Kate a safe trip." Gran shook her head. "Going to Disney World."

"I'll come in with you. Oh, did Daisy spill the beans to you?"

"What beans?"

"Figure of speech, Gran. She said she's going to be a bridesmaid."

"A bridesmaid?"

"Um hum. She said that Finn and her mommy are going to get married in Sleeping Beauty's Castle. Something about spending a few bitcoins."

The End

Author's Note

It seems Jane and Danny's dream is materializing. The transformation of the homestead into business centers. And now, their growing family is embracing the establishment of a brewpub.

Who is Rosemary? First, Sadie finds a picture in the attic of the farmhouse. The name *Rosemary* is written on the back. And now a hymnal inscribed to Rosemary, is found in a very different place on the farm. What to make of it?

PS: Many readers to date have asked about the Prologue in book one. The baby in a basket left at a church, who was the mother, whose skull did Dog unearth? A few clues have surfaced, or have they? Are they connected? We'll find the answers together. Of course, I can't promise more questions won't arise along the way.

You must excuse me again. I have to run. Jeli is pestering me about her appointment with a developer in Boston. She says it may be her big chance to put her design talents to work. I'll have to see about that!

Acknowledgements

A big shout out to the following for their unique contributions:

Tomoka Farm Craft Brewery, Rich McCarthy, partner. Partners, Pete Szunyogh and Jen Hawkins, Master Brewer and Brewster

Tumbleweed, Tiny House Company, HGTV. Mike Nelson, Cassie O'Mara. Mike's passion for home brewing was the inspiration for duel role of the Cameron Foster character. TumbleweedHouses.com

Brian Kelly, Brian Kelly Capital, CNBC Contributor, Fast Money Commentator. Brian Kelly, author: *The Bitcoin Big Bang: How Alternative Currencies Are About to change the World,* Nov. 17, 2014. Publisher: Wiley.

Start Your Own Microbrewery, Distillery, or Cidery, The Staff of Entrepreneur Media, Inc. Entrepreneur Press, Publisher, eBook, 2015.

Geri and Dick Rogers, thank you for helping with the research at the brewery—very tasty.

Carlton Keeney, thank you for the character name, Jeli.

Kudos, as always, to my reviewers:
Molly Tredwell—big picture
Peggy Keeney—constantly digging deeper and deeper
Roger and Pat Grady—at all times, giving a fresh perspective

About the Author

Mary Jane retired to Florida where she penned her first novel, "Murder in the House of Beads." While she has written three short stories, her novels fall under the genre: Cozy Romance Mysteries.

She says her writing has been, and continues to be, an incredible journey. In researching her books she's met many wonderful people who shared insights on the tools of their trade as well as their experiences which were intriguing, inspiring and very educational.

Case in point, chatting with the Tomoka Brewing Company partners over a glass of McCarthy's Irish Red Ale; and, correspondence with several staff members at Tumbleweed, Tiny House Company.

Writing about topics currently in the news, she hopes her stories will add perspective and insight. FINN shines a spotlight on the tiny house craze spreading across the country, as well as craft brewpubs, and bitcoins (a cryptocurrency).

Mary Jane graduated from the University of Utah, and owned and operated a computer school for ten years in Newburyport, Massachusetts. She resides in Port Orange, Florida—a writing paradise.

Books by Mary Jane Forbes

Bradley Farm Series
The Bradley Farm
Sadie, Finn, Jeli
Marshall, Georgie

The Baker Girl Series
One Summer
Promises

Twists of Fate Series
The Fisherman, a love story
The Witness, living a lie
Twists of Fate

Murder by Design Series:
Murder by Design
Labeled in Seattle
Choices, And the Courage to Risk

Novels
The Mailbox
Black Magic, An Arabian Stallion
The Painter
The Baby Quilt ... a mystery!
The Message...Call Me!
Twister

House of Beads Mystery Series
Murder in the House of Beads
Intercept
Checkmate
Identity Theft

Short Stories
Once Upon a Christmas Eve, a Romantic Fairy Tale
The Christmas Angel and the Magic Holiday Tree
RJ, The Little Hero

Visit: www.MaryJaneForbes.com

NEXT BOOK IN SERIES
JELI, Bradley Farm Series Book 4

A promising project. A deadly hidden secret. Can one interior designer catch the killer before her career is dead on arrival?

With a splash of paint and the perfect signature piece, Jeli Bradley can transform any apartment into a work of art. Despite her talent, she can't find a client willing to take a chance on an untested designer. When a brash young contractor taps her to decorate his Boston condo complex, she eagerly takes on the trial project... despite her complete ignorance of the Asian-inspired aesthetic.

Determined to win the bid, she immerses herself in traditional Chinese design, catching the eye of both her new boss and a condo financer's handsome grandson. But when the building's first resident is found murdered, Jeli's career-defining design teeters on the edge of collapse. To keep the project on track, the designer must navigate a web of dark secrets and crooked investors. With her career riding on an unstable deck of cards, Jeli has no choice but to solve the case before everything comes crashing down.

Jeli is the fourth standalone romantic mystery in the compelling Bradley Farm family saga series. If you like spunky heroines, stunning home makeovers, and riveting suspense, then you'll love Mary Jane Forbes' high-rise whodunit.!

BRADLEY FARM SERIES

.

www.ingramcontent.com/pod-product-compliance
Lightning Source LLC
Chambersburg PA
CBHW070817120626
46556CB00002B/550